SINSEMILLA BOOTLEGGER

# SINSEMILLA
# BOOTLEGGER

## PAUL KALMAN

COUNCIL OAK BOOKS
OAKLAND, CALIFORNIA

Photo credits: The Colorado courtesy Harlan Ang © 2012
Jack Herer courtesy Green House Seeds
Cannalope-Haze courtesy DNA Genetics
Fuma Con Dios courtesy Flying Dutchmen Seeds
All other pictures courtesy Paul Kalman © 2012

Printed and Bound in Canada
10 9 8 7 6 5 4 3 2 1

First Edition

Library of Congress Cataloging-in-Publication Data
has been applied for

ISBN-13 978-1571783202

Photographs © 2012
Illustrations © Jim Welch 2012
Cover Design & Layout © Jim Welch 2012
Interior Design by Blue Design

Council Oak Books
2225 Campbell Street
Oakland, California
94607

www.counciloakbooks.com

Distributed by Publishers Group West

*Follow these words where they lead*
*and I will meet you in the garden.*

*In Joy,*
*Paul Kalman*

## ACKNOWLEDGEMENTS

Thanks due to Mary Kalman for being hot and for her help editing, to Summer and Jazmine for being the coolest and Herbie & The Philosophers Club for further inspiration. Also, to Nadine Condon, my cheerleader, Jim Welch for cover art heroics, Pat Johnson and Harvey Mandell for picture magic, Amy Glazer and James Connolly for direction, and Linda Foust for editing.

Special thanks to those friends, family and acquaintances whose descriptions and escapades I have appropriated for this tale. I have changed your names to protect the guilty, but you know who you are.

(Raven, Donal, Dan, Mary, Haj, Wayne, Dude, Terri, Jimmy, Kevin, Lamar, Don, and Eddie)

*This book is dedicated to Gene and Bernice Kalman.*
*Nothing would be right in this world without your love.*

# CHAPTER 1

I could feel it before I heard it. As it drew closer, my pulse rate quickened until I could positively identify the roar of a train going by. It was a normal occurrence. Just about every night around ten that train passed, and after eight weeks I was getting used to it. But this time there was something different. And then, as the train faded, I heard it. A police siren, close, rising out of the clamor of the train, as though it were trying to sneak up on me. Instant injected adrenalin. Then the voice of the Narrator in my head: "The next sound you hear will be the beating of your own heart."

In an instant, I calculated all the options. Not too difficult a task, seeing as I'd been mulling over the possibilities for almost a year and still hadn't come up with any, save one small hiding place that they would probably find anyway. Once again, the crushing reality set in. Nowhere to run. An unnerving prospect for those of us used to growing our illicit crop in the sunshine of California's backwoods. But inside that nonstop marijuana mill, there was no off-season and no pressure drop at harvest time. If not for moments like that I could probably have maintained my Johnny Potseed self-image all the time, but fear had a way of shattering my hero fantasy to bits.

For growers, tending one of those glowing gardens in a locked box was a torture test for true believers only, but that climate-controlled environment was actually an oasis. Outside, there was a war waging, a crack war, between a community forced to feed on itself for its very survival and a society that believed the answer to poverty was more prisons. Used syringes and empty crack vials were commonplace on the walk outside, and the police seemed to have established a free-fire zone in response to the attempt by well-armed, well-financed youth to lift themselves up by their bootstraps and beat a path out of the ghetto, a path well worn by most profiteers of American dreaming, leaving only wreckage and ruined lives in their wake.

The adrenalin rush left my body a quivering mass of Jell-O, inside my head a full production of paranoid theater, but out there twelve-year-olds run from the blue meanies totally unaffected by my moment of exaggerated paranoia.

Then the voice brought me back: "Four lights, times one-and-a-quarter pounds at three thousand dollars each." The Narrator hadn't left the room. Even as I side-tripped on this mind-bending detour, the Narrator stayed behind to figure the profits of the night's harvest. Firmly rooted in my here and now, the Narrator had an uncanny third person's perspective. Like a camera in my mind's eye, focused on me, he offered awareness of the present.

The lights went on about two hours earlier. I didn't breath for fifteen minutes, then I loosened up and, after a short period of time—about as long as it takes to harvest two lights—I was bouncing along to Mother's Finest wailing away on the stereo.

Harvesting was not a difficult job. In fact, it was the best job on the whole project. Eventually, I'd forget completely where I was. It all seemed perfectly natural, even in that sterile environment. Call me a spiritual fool, but there was something righteous about this plant. Was it some cosmic, hippy-dippy trip, or the old rebellious outlaw thing? Maybe it was just the money, and I was kidding myself, an auto-con. Anyway, another hour or so and the harvest ritual was over, and then I made my way over to post-op, a drying and trimming facility at another location. The whole ceremony was rather anticlimactic, seeing as I had done it the week before, and the next week it needed to be done again.

✳   ✳   ✳   ✳   ✳   ✳   ✳

The last flashes of afternoon sunlight through the oak trees outside the window caught my eyes and gently awakened me. The familiar sound of scampering paws across the wood-shingle roof drew my attention to the far corner of the house, just in time to catch the Flying Squirrelendas—a local family of squirrels—as they made the death-defying five-foot leap into the oak trees that virtually surrounded Charlie's house. Charlie, Carlotta Micos, owned the house and lived there with a friend. I wasn't a roommate but you wouldn't have known it, because I was kind of a fixture around there.

Nestled under the oak trees at the end of Shady Lane, "the hideout," as I called it, had been my place of refuge for almost a year. I rarely went back to the storefront apartment in Berkeley that I shared with Winston, a good friend, who had been playing his guitar on the Oakland/Berkeley blues circuit since '71, when he graduated from high school. There wasn't any fame or fortune involved, but the scene was rich in tradition, going back to the thirties when Oakland had over a hundred blues clubs and more blues musicians than any town this side of Chicago.

Until Charlie cuddled up a little closer, I didn't realize she was there. She hadn't been home when I got there that morning. She must have come in and fallen asleep on the couch beside me. I kissed her on the cheek, and as soon as she awoke, her hands began to massage my chest. The girl's hands never stopped. Without conscious thought, they soothed whatever they touched.

"Hi, darlin," she said, looking up with a sleepy smile.

"When did you get in?" I asked.

"About an hour ago. I had to deal with Tina Wilson's irate husband, a lawyer from the city, who couldn't understand why I won't tell him where his wife is so he can go beat her up again."

"Were you able to get through to him?"

"He was so busy being threatening and abusive that even I couldn't break through. He said all the nasty shit he could think of, and when he ran out of words, he turned to throwing rocks through the windows at the shelter. Then he proceeded to take his anger out on the front quarter-panel of my car."

"Uh-oh. Is he okay?"

"Jason, what do you mean is he okay? What about Tina? What about the shelter? What about my car?"

"I mean, what hospital is he in?" I said, half-seriously.

"Very funny. He even threatened to kill Tina right in front of a cop, the idiot. The cop just put him back in his fancy aqua blue Mercedes and sent him on his merry way. Needless to say, the cop was a man also."

That guy obviously didn't know Carlotta very well. I'll admit, Charlie's features are not physically threatening, with long, thick, dirty-blond hair, and hypnotic green eyes set in a slender, five-foot-five-inch, 110-pound frame. Though she could be sexually intimidating, looks like that didn't reveal how dangerous she really was.

The first time I met Charlie, she was sitting buried up to her waist in wet *kolas*. She ran a trimming operation for a co-op of growers in a rundown house on one-hundred-eighty acres outside of Leggett that belonged to her grandmother. A dazzling twenty-year-old fireball in blue jeans and boots. It was 1982, and the California grower was turning out thousands of pounds of the absolutely best reefer the world has known at prices that were so low

almost everyone could smoke the best. She took in wet plant from
several different growers, then dried it, trimmed it, priced and sold it
with her crew of so-called housewives. In 1983, they trimmed close
to eight hundred pounds. During the season, the ladies often grossed
much more than their husbands, who risked their health in the mill
year after year.

We spent the next few years together, traveling the high road. At
one end was the deceiving tranquility of the emerald woods, where
quiet and hard working citizens lived a small-town life. Meanwhile,
back in the high manzanita behind the house, they worked the soil for
a living in the true entrepreneurial spirit. Contrary to popular thought,
most growers earned a realistic sum. Thirty thousand dollars wasn't a
huge amount to make for a year's work, but you did get it all at once.

We grew a small garden together just inside the national forest in
Trinity County. A ten-plant guerrilla patch that we put in near our
favorite swimming hole at Salt Creek. We spent one day of every week
there tending the garden.

Charlie had a penchant for debauchery, but she could always keep
herself together no matter how rowdy she got. Her operation was not
a small responsibility, and with her newfound talent for distribution,
namely me, she began to suck up all the pot in the neighborhood. She
middled for lots of growers, but close to a dozen of them gave her wet
plant. They trusted her to tell them how much it weighed and to set
the price.

But on those days at Salt Creek, Charlie turned loose. We left my
van, the Mobile Hilton, about 8:00 a.m. at the trail's head where the
county road crosses the creek, about an hour's walk from the swimming
hole. Donning our packs and splitting a Quaalude, we hiked into the
hidden, granite canyon. After setting up a small camp for the day,
we left our gear and walked another mile through the bush to our
well-hidden string of plants. Charlie kept the Quaaludes and coke
coming in small amounts all day long. She loved to seduce me in our

garden full of frustrated female plants. She would make love to me as if in a trance, unbridled passion, wild and primal. In the deep woods, we were able to cast off our inhibitions like dirty clothes and show off our true selves without fear of disapproval.

We spent the rest of the day at the pool, a thirty-yard-long, natural hole in the granite. Even in late summer when the creek went dry, this water paradise with forty-foot cliff dives, twenty-foot granite rockslides, and a resident eight-inch turtle named Jake would remain like an oasis.

We used those as get-away days, but most of our time in the north country was spent beating the bushes for *ganja*. She processed it through her machine, and I piped it to the streets, a flood of green gold. We stole over the back roads like modern-day bootleggers and ran the highways back to Berkeley so often that our cars knew the way by heart.

Like Salt Creek, Berkeley was also an oasis. In this cozy counterculture, surrounded by a ravenous metropolis, the Woodstock nation hung on. The system gobbled up the idea of long hair, better living through chemistry, and rock and roll and spit it back out as twenty-five-dollar haircuts, speed, and The Monkees. But the tribe lived on in Berkeley and other enclaves around the country. After being crushed in the streets—being beaten, busted, and buried—they retreated, only to suffer a whole generation of reaction. The evil Governor Reagan became king, and the me-decade was a moral defeat. At last, the king was gone, and now, twenty years later, they wondered if it was safe to slip off their hats freeing long, bushy hair to grow "down to where it stops by itself." Like a bear waking from a long hibernation searching for honey, they poked their heads out of their caves and sniffed the air for faint traces of patchouli oil.

And there were signs to take solace in. After all, tie-dye and leather fringe were in style again. There was a folk song in the top one hundred. The Dead had the biggest box office of any band on the road, and David

Crosby lived. All the battles of yesteryear were left unwon, and the soldiers who fought them were still out there, somewhere. Millions of Americans were in the street, and millions more so-called discouraged workers went uncounted. Yet there was no trigger, no spark. Twenty years before, there was the outrage of Vietnam to rally against, and yes, Virginia, there was an Owsley.

After a couple of years, Charlie moved to the city. She stayed with me for a couple of months until she made friends with Angela, who worked with the Battered Women's Underground. They made it their job to shelter and hide if necessary, women who lived in fear of their ex-husbands or boyfriends. Many were running scared with few places to turn. Some were afraid of having their children stolen from them. Most were just through being beaten. A whole network of people around the country had offered their homes and their help to these women, even though the authorities in this country were often on the side of the men.

Charlie fit perfectly with this resolute group of women, devoted to their cause regardless of legalities or consequences. She was well-schooled in clandestine activities, and her friends in the country welcomed quite a few ladies into the community over the next year.

I wanted Charlie to stay with me, but she was determined to be on her own. And she could afford it. In fact, she had trimmed enough pot to put a down-payment on the hideout, and she and Angela moved in. I'd say there wasn't anything she couldn't do.

It was two Salvadorian ladies who were staying at the shelter that got her involved with aid to El Salvador. After six months of raising money for medical care and finding places for refugees to stay, she tired of passive measures and began to raise money for a trunk-load of guns. I tried to reason with her, but it was no use. She said she felt it was very much the same as growing pot. It was good for the planet. She saw both as blows against the empire.

I worried out loud for an hour, uninterrupted. I made great argu-ments as to the futility of it. "Today's revolution is tomorrow's *coup* is the next day's right-wing dictatorship," I said. As to the danger of a beautiful woman traveling the Pan American Highway, "It's a job better suited to a man, and there are other valuable ways of making a contribution." I even tried a direct attack, "Those people don't need you to tell them how to fight a revolution. Your time would be better spent working on the struggle in your own country, at the root of the problem."

She let me go on for quite a while, patiently listening until I was spent, and then replied, "You don't believe a word of that crap." As usual, with x-ray vision, she looked right through me, and, with a scalpel-sharp tongue, surgically removed my argument. She was right. But, unfazed by facts, I began to try again. "Your Spanish is not good enough to get you through Mexico and Guatemala..."

This time she interrupted. "You're so cute when you worry about me." Frustrated, I collapsed in the big sofa-chair. She climbed onto my lap, facing me, and began tugging at my shirt. "I know how concerned you are, and I'm glad, but the trip isn't for another month. I'll think carefully about what you've said, but there isn't any more you can do." With that said, she kissed me, and all further discussion ceased. Actually, it was the gentle kisses that she placed on my neck that caused me to lose concentration completely.

Two weeks later, we made a run up north to harvest the Salt Creek garden for the second straight year. What a spot. When we returned, we trimmed it up, and Charlie sold it all. She collected slightly over sixteen-thousand dollars. On the night she sold out, we popped a twenty-year-old bottle of cabernet to celebrate our successful garden. Then we shared a fantastic meal that we prepared together at the hideout. After dividing the money and the stash buds we had saved for ourselves, there was one fifty-dollar bill left-over.

"I leave for Mexico day after tomorrow," she said.

"There's nothing I can say to stop you?"

"No."

"Then I want to tell you how I really feel about it." She seemed uneasy. "The truth is, I have a lot of respect for what you're doing, not to mention your courage to follow up your convictions with action. I've tried to put myself in your shoes. I asked myself what I would expect from you if it were me going to Central America. So let me say this. I love you more than I ever thought I could love someone, and I'm just now getting to the point where that doesn't scare me. So keep yourself healthy for the both of us and come home soon, or I'm going down there to look for you."

"I love you too, baby," she said. Then she tore the fifty in half. "Here, you take this half, and when I get back we'll go out and blow it together." Amazing woman!

We didn't get out of bed the whole next day. We watched the football games, pigged out on junk food, and made love straight into the night. When I woke up the following morning, the phone was ringing. Groggy, I picked up the receiver, but I hesitated before answering. I could tell Charlie was gone, and by the size of the bag she had packed, it would be awhile before I'd see her face again.

Bringgg, bringgg. I heard the telephone ringing, but I was slow to respond. Bringgg, bringgg. "Answer the phone, you idiot." It was the Narrator again, mercilessly jolting me out of a whirlpool of self-pity.

"Hello?"

# CHAPTER 2

**H**ello?"

"Hi, pal." I hadn't heard that voice in a long time. Only one person on this planet has ever called me "pal." This salutation is his way of identifying himself without using names. I remember our last conversation word for word. It was two years before, and the usually dispassionate voice was slightly panicked. He told me not to trust any of our mutual friends, that he had "some trouble." He would not be in touch, and I shouldn't try to contact him.

I asked him if there was any way I could help. He said I could take the white Cadillac that he had been driving that week to the Co-op parking lot in Berkeley and put the keys in the left rear wheel well. It was parked at his apartment, and he wasn't going back. Since then, I hadn't heard from him, and although we were close friends, somehow I hadn't expected to.

Chester Hawthorne was the most mysterious character I'd ever known. Every time I saw him coming, I knew that adventure and

trouble weren't far behind. He grew up the son of a highly placed
C.I.A. agent stationed in Berlin. His father was military attaché to
the consulate there in the early sixties, and Chester had to be escorted
by military police to private English-speaking schools throughout his
early teens.

In the mid-sixties, his father became chief of covert operations in
Saigon, and Chet came back to the family homestead in Maryland.
After finishing high school in '68, he enrolled in George Washington
University, where his older brother was already attending college. It
was there, while his father was still in Vietnam, that he began to feel
disdain for the Washington capital ethic that he was raised in.

He joined Students for a Democratic Society (S.D.S.) and began
to apply the intelligence and undercover skills that had been passed
on to him in his genes. And he was good at it. His father should have
been proud. Ironically, it was the first major break with the family.
Mr. Hawthorne had had problems with his son since the eighth grade,
when Chet began wearing sandals and stopped cutting his hair. Like so
many other American kids of the time, he rejected the establishment,
but his father, more than all others, represented all that was evil about
the system, and inevitably the split would come.

Late in 1971, his father received an urgent call to return to
Washington. Chester was busted with 150,000 hits of acid and
eighty-five thousand in cash. He had been flying out to Berkeley to
score about twice a month for half a year and he claimed to have
distributed three-quarters of a million doses. The feds were ready to
make a major case out of the bust until his dad showed up in the nick
of time. He got his son off the hook, but Chet lost everything in the
process—$200,000 in seizures, legal fees, and fines. He also lost his
father's respect and was branded the black sheep of the family. Broke
and alone, he put his guitar and amp in the back seat of his two-toned
Karmann Ghia convertible and headed for Berkeley in 1972.

Six years later, he was back at it, moving thousands of pounds of high-grade Mexican spears from Pueblo and Oaxaca. His operation ran like a many-geared clock, and he kept it tightly wound. He would fly into the fields in Mexico and pick out the ones he wanted while the plants were still in the ground. Leaving the smuggling up to the Mexicans, he arranged to buy it in California. Once it was safely warehoused, his crew would meticulously repackage everything and then disburse it over the western states and D.C.

But the unique thing he did was to save the seeds in the heavily seeded tops and sell them, by weight, to growers he knew in the Midwest for about twice what he paid for them. I saw him turn over gallon Ziploc bags full of seeds, literally hundreds of thousands of seeds. At $250 per pound, it wasn't a great deal of profit, but it was essential for the growers, and in my opinion, downright righteous.

It was seeds that brought us together. I had been buying pot from him through a mutual friend who told him about a strain of extremely strong Indica seeds that I was selling for one dollar each. I had five-thousand of them that came out of some Colorado-grown buds I bought from a stereotypical San Francisco street-freak named Easy. He was anything but. I managed to convince him that his buds weren't worth top dollar—two-thousand dollars per pound—because they were so heavily seeded. I paid $1,650 each for four pounds of the meanest smoke I've ever had before or since.

When Chet saw a sample of those hard-rock buds and the seeds that came out of them, he got very interested in me. He bought all five thousand seeds, and I made him pay the full price. After all, at the time, I was selling a pound here and a half-pound there, and he was moving thousands of pounds per month. He said I was price-gouging him and that later he would find a way to make me pay, but really I think I gained not only his money, but his respect.

Later that year, I grew my first large guerrilla crop up north with two close doobie brothers, my right-hand man and sidekick for many years, Jungle Jim, and my main supplier in Leggett, Afghan Dan. We grew sixty pounds from my Colorado seeds. We called it "L & L," Love and Luck, and we sold it for twenty-five hundred a pound, and in 1979 that was three or four hundred over top dollar.

All growers truly believe their stash to be the best. Suffice to say, the L & L was flat impressive weed, and everyone who planted those seeds got comparable results. The following winter, *High Times* published pictures of the original Colorado buds and a great shot of the seeds on a red-velvet background. Word began to spread quickly throughout the Emerald Triangle. Demand for these seeds became overwhelming, while the supply was nonexistent. Those few growers who had access to Indica seeds guarded them like precious stones. You'd have been lucky to find an ounce of lightly seeded Indica. Even then, it would cost six-hundred dollars. I did have a couple thousand stashed away, but I had no intention of giving them up. The only other person I knew who had Colorado seeds was Chet, but he managed to sell all his to the Midwestern growers for a whopping 100% profit. In fact, he was quite anxious to get more from me so he could expand on what he felt would be the future of the marijuana business.

Meanwhile, Chet and I became fast friends. He was a marijuana secret agent with all the tricks and tools of the trade. I called him Dope Tracy. The guy actually wore a dress, teardrop-shaped, felt hat and trench coat and smoked Gauloises. He wore a pair of wire-framed glasses like John Lennon's, except his darkened in sunlight. For the first year I knew him, he was never in the same car twice. He had stash houses with built-in hidden rooms, cars built to bootleg, phone systems, machines and beepers, and all the latest in electronic gadgets, like radar detectors, and two-way and police-band radios. He even had some surveillance equipment, like motion detectors, voice-activated tape, and an FM directional receiver acquired from his "uncles," long-time friends of his father that he still stayed in touch with.

He paid very close attention to small details, but he really thought big. I, on the other hand, was a kid with a thriving retail business carelessly speeding the wrong way down a one-way street towards being busted or ripped off. Easy pickin's for any halfway-serious cop or criminal. But Chet straightened me out. He gave me a bale of Columbian on credit, knowing full well I couldn't sell that much. He said, "Just put it in your closet and pay me when you can." With him as my supplier and mentor I was set, but I would have to follow his rules. Eventually, I did sell it, then another and another, until retail became wholesale, and I learned the rules of the game.

\*　　\*　　\*　　\*　　\*　　\*　　\*

About two months before planting time, I got a call from Easy. He wanted to meet me at a friend's house in San Francisco about a block from the Panhandle. By this time, I was well aware of the value of good seeds. The previous year, we sold all the seeded Colorado buds, and people just threw the seeds away. When I went to meet Easy, I took Chet with me. He was an ominous presence lurking wordlessly in the background.

Easy was *un*easy, as was Chet. After all, here he was in a stranger's house doing business with Easy, who was a flake, at best, and a definite security risk. Father would not approve of such a sloppy operation. But risk or not, Easy came through again. Twenty-six pounds of the same weed, chock full of ripe seeds. I complained again about the seed weight and the price, but Easy and I both knew I was gonna buy all I could afford. After about an hour, I spent every penny I had on eight pounds.

Then, for the first time, Chet took off his coat and sat down. He tore open the Velcro seam he had sewn into the lining of his coat and pulled out forty grand, enough to buy the rest of the load. Then he produced two duffle bags from his briefcase and stuffed them with buds, while Easy and I gleefully counted the money.

I wanted to spread these seeds all over the California countryside to all the growers I knew and all the growers they knew, thereby guaranteeing myself a steady, high-quality supply. As ye sow, so shall ye reap. That would require twenty thousand seeds, at most, over a three-or-four-year period, only three pounds. But we had just purchased over two-hundred-thousand seeds and paid $2,000 a pound for pot that was more than half seed and stem. Obviously, Chet had a plan, and I hoped it was a good one.

I made it to the north country right before spring planting. All my friends were very happy to see me. I sold Colorado seeds to every farmer I knew for one dollar each. It couldn't have been more than six thousand seeds total, but Chet took the seeded buds and a sample of my L & L to the Midwest and Mexico and returned with orders for forty-thousand seeds at full price. And he kept it up for four of the next five years.

We kept all the seeds in the bottom of the bags and all of the most mature buds. The rest of the weed we sold in Los Angeles, knowing those seeds would be discarded. Then began the task of deseeding seventeen pounds of heavily seeded indica. I crushed and cleaned seven pounds the month after Chet got back from Mexico, then culled out six Mason jars full of the finest seed stock ever available. For this grueling effort, I got to keep the six-to-seven ounces per pound of bud shake that was left over.

I loved selling seeds, providing thousands of them to growers in different locations throughout the country. When I couldn't sell a thousand, I gave away a hundred. I even gave three thousand to a Rasta named Joseph I met in Jamaica on a small, white sand beach just south of Negril. Joseph assured me that I'd be paid after harvest. Fat chance. But I was more interested in boosting the quality of their product. After all, every time I rolled a joint, thirty-dollars-worth of seeds rained out. It was like being paid to get high.

Although I respected Chester Hawthorne for his insight and experience, for his uniquely cynical slant on life with a paranoid twist, what I really loved was the Dick Tracy-like comic-strip hero he portrayed. One time he swapped fifty thousand seeds for thirty pounds of pot from the Midwest Combine. By then, they had harvested three crops of well over five hundred pounds each. Why they never grew their own seeds I'll never understand. Year after year, they returned to buy tens of thousands of them.

After that deal, the only communication I received was that one panicked call. But now the sounds of his happy, "Hi, pal," relieved all of my fears that something terrible had happened.

"Hi, pal," I answered. "I've been missing you. Are you okay?"

"Yeah, I'm fine. And I'm back in town," he said.

"Great! What happened before you left?"

"I'll tell you when I see you. Meet me in spot number three."

"Okay. What time?" I already knew his answer.

"Well, what time do you think?"

"Right now?"

"That's right."

"Okay, I'm already gone. Bye."

I loved this I-Spy stuff. I said goodbye, but I think the phone was already on the hook. Spot number three was one of five pre-arranged meeting places. He also had the phone numbers of at least twenty different pay phones that he used for receiving calls. Number three was a *hofbrau* at the foot of University called Brennan's. He liked the spot because it had a rich history of being a meeting place for Berkeley middlemen in the seventies.

When I got to Brennan's, Chet was in his usual spot, all the way in the far corner of the large room with his back to the wall, reading the paper. He was wearing a stylish jogging outfit that must have cost a hundred-and-fifty bucks. He carried a workout bag and looked like he had just come from a racquetball game with the guys at the office, but I knew better. I wondered what was in the bag.

This thought reminded me of how in character Chet always was. When he saw me approaching, a big smile dawned on his face, a welcome memory. As he lowered the newspaper, I caught a glimpse of the two necklaces he wore. One had a one-ounce pyramid of gold dangling from it. Beside the pyramid, hung a one-inch-long naked woman made of gold with an incredibly small diamond in her crotch. I couldn't see what was on the other chain, but I knew what it was. A very lightweight and very sharp three-inch blade in a quick-release plastic sheath. Chet was always armed with two or three weapons, though I never saw him use them on anyone. They were everywhere—in his car, in his bag, at his house, and always something on his person. He had fancy pellet guns and wrist rockets and blackjacks and lots of police equipment, like handcuffs, an electric shocker, and a billy-club flashlight, as well as several handguns and dozens of fancy knives. At six-one and one-hundred-and-eighty pounds I was considerably bigger than he, but I would never have tried to take him on.

"Hi, pal," he said, standing to give me a big hug.

"Hi. I was really worried about you. What happened?"

"Oh, someone ripped off my stock and even found my personal stash."

"From the built-in spot under the house? No one could possibly have found that spot," I said.

"That's right. No one except you and Patrick knew about it."

Patrick was Chet's right-hand man. When I first began working with him, Chet told me I could trust Patrick with anything. He knew every meeting place and hiding spot and often ran things when Chet was away.

"Well, you called me before you took off, so I assume that means you suspect Patrick," I said.

"There isn't any other possibility, Jason," he replied. "That is why you're the only person who knows that I'm back."

"Where is Patrick now? What are you going to do about it?"

"Well, do you remember Sean?" he asked.

"Yes, you introduced me to him about a year ago, but he seemed like a pretty sleazy character."

"That's him. He's a slimeball, but the guy is a born spook. I've got him keeping an eye on Patrick for me. Patrick lives in San Francisco now with his girlfriend. He hasn't been spending a lot of money or selling anything, but Sean is real close to him, and if anything changes, he'll send word to me in D.C. He still thinks I'm there. Then a friend in D.C. gets back to me here."

"Are we going after Patrick?" I expected him to be planning his revenge.

"You mean, am I going to hurt him? No. There are three choices, as always, in matters of this sort. I can seek revenge, in which case I get the satisfaction and little else. I can set aside revenge and keep a thriving business alive, or I can watch and wait and hope to find an opportunity to do both."

"Is that why you're here?" I asked.

"No. I've got something else going, and I need your help."

"I've got something good going also," I told him. "I've moved my gardens indoors. I have twenty-two lights going now, and I'm building another sixteen-light setup that should come on line in about three or four months."

"How long have you been doing that?"

"Since a little under a year before you disappeared."

"You never mentioned anything about that before I left," he said.

"Well, you always taught me that it was more fun to keep a secret than to tell it."

"So I did. How are you doing with it?" he asked.

"We can produce between three and five-thousand dollars per light six times a year. We have eighteen bloom lights going now and twelve more coming."

I could see the calculator going off in his head. His lips quietly multiplied the figures. Quickly, he reached the bottom line.

"That's around three-quarters of a million annually!"

"Yep," I agreed. "Subtract one-hundred-thousand in expenses and divide by three partners, and you'll still get a great return."

"That is fantastic! What did it take to get set up?"

"About fifty-thousand and about eight months, but I can do it faster and cheaper now."

"And the risk?" he asked.

"Well, that's the worst part. We harvest every week, all year long. It never ends. The cops are shooting themselves in the foot with this CAMP thing. After three years of choppers and storm troops, the whole pot-growing community has gone inside. Now, instead of having the growers in a few small areas harvesting one crop in October and selling it by the end of January, they have growers spread all over the country, harvesting six cycles a year and creating a nonstop supply. And the technology is leaping forward. Soon we predict that we can raise our production per light by about thirty percent, and by the time they start directing their attention towards indoors, we'll have our new outdoor scheme perfected."

"And what's that?"

"Spikes," I answered. "Cloned female plants put in after the planes fly that only grow to two feet, taking a mere seven or eight weeks to mature. When we perfect it, we will be able to reactivate at least half of the outdoor gardens that they presently have shut down."

"Boy, you have been busy. I see you've learned to look far into the future."

"Another lesson I picked up from you." I said.

"When do I get to see it?" he asked.

"I'll have to ask my partners. It's been a long time, and I haven't told a soul until now. What's up with you?"

"Well, as you know, my guys out of state took last year off. Those guys have incredible luck. The one year they didn't plant, we had a brutal drought. It would surely have wrecked their crop. Anyway, they say this will be their last year, and they put in an order for sixty thousand seeds."

"My God!"

"That's right. At four-to-one, that's fifteen-thousand females grown out in God's golden sun."

"Our seeds have had it," I said. "Where are we going to get sixty thousand seeds? We've been growing a powerful strain we call "The Weed That Killed Elvis" that they would love, but we run the whole project on cloned cuttings. There are no seeds."

"That's your department, pal," he smiled. "I'm sure that with your resources in the woods, you can handle it."

"I'll be able to come up with some, but sixty-thousand will take some doing," I said.

"Then do it," he replied without hesitation.

"How much are they willing to spend?"

"They think they should be able to get away with less than a buck each."

"They better think again. They'll cost us at least a buck. Is there any room for us to make money on that?"

"Well, the way I figure it, if this is their last year, and they will probably be the biggest game in town next season, we should cut them the best deal possible and collect our profit in gratitude later."

"What if they don't make it?" I asked.

"Then we haven't lost much in comparison to what we stand to gain. My question is, can we get our hands on sixty-thousand good seeds?"

"These days most people who have a good place to grow don't waste it on seeded pot," I said. "Plus, we don't have a good idea of what kind of strain we're buying. We gave a money-back guarantee with our seeds, but we can't do that if we're going to buy them from an assortment of different growers."

"Well, look into it and let me know what you find out. Here is my new service number. It's under this name. Be discrete, as always. I have to go. Sorry I split so abruptly, but it's really good to see you again."

He handed me a slip of paper with the number on it. The name was Casey Williams, a take-off on William Casey, our present Director of Central Intelligence.

"It's great to have you back. I'll get right on this and call you."

"Good. Take care."

"You do the same, buddy."

Chet pushed aside the newspaper, picked up his bag, and left. I watched him go. I would wait a few minutes before leaving. As I turned my attention back to the table, I was shocked to see the picture and headline on page three of the open paper in front of me. The picture was of what was left of an aqua-blue Mercedes, and the headline read, "Attorney Hospitalized after Auto Bombed."

# CHAPTER 3

*"San Francisco attorney William Wilson was
hospitalized yesterday at San Francisco General
Hospital when, after parking and exiting his
vehicle, it exploded behind him. Police say the
equivalent of two sticks of dynamite were
detonated by radio remote at about four p.m.
yesterday outside Mr. Wilson's home. There are
no suspects in the case, and Mr. Wilson refuses to
talk to the police. After his release from San
Francisco General late last night, Mr. Wilson
avoided the media by slipping out the side
entrance and is still unavailable for comment."*

I was only half-joking when I asked Carlotta what hospital that
guy was in. I knew her too well to go for that shit about not being as
bad as the other guy. If this was her doing, it would go beyond even

my estimation of her capability for direct action, but I was absolutely positive that it was her doing. I saw a direct connection between this Wilson character denting Charlie's car and the explosion of his prized auto. That sounded like Charlie. Retaliate in kind, tenfold. Not to mention that she just happened to be on her way out of the country.

I returned to the hideout to see if I could find some answers to the questions posed by Chet. On the news that evening, reporters had made some connection between the shelter incident and the car bomb. They interviewed a woman from the shelter whom I did not know. However, she was typical of those I did know. Straightforward, she stuck to the shelter's line.

"The Battered Women's Underground does not condone this or any act of violence. We have nothing to do with violence. On the contrary, we protect the lives of abused women and children who seek a way out of violent situations.

"Mr. Wilson is the perfect example of what we're up against. Not surprisingly, a wealthy male lawyer has been able to convince Judge Perkins, another wealthy male lawyer, to give him visitation rights and weekends with his eight-year-old daughter. It was clear from the testimony that both Mrs. Wilson and her daughter were beaten and abused. Nevertheless, Judge Perkins declared Mr. Wilson fit. Mrs. Wilson has no intention of giving her child to this man, and, to this end, we at the shelter will stand behind her.

"We have a great respect for the laws of this country. However, we feel that the legal system has fallen far short of justice in regard to this and other women's issues. We will not abandon our sisters, no matter the cost. That will be our only statement. Thank you."

There wasn't any mention of Charlie, but I decided to leave the hideout, my only place of refuge, anyway. I packed my bag the next day and went back to Winston's apartment in the heart of Berkeley. The pressure seemed to be building. Two days later, I had to harvest and plant again, about twenty-five hours work. Then two days of trimming before an off week. I needed to escape.

I couldn't take it at Winston's place. Dozens of street people coming and going—a virtual flea market for illicit drugs and other potions not yet illegal, concocted by tinkering chemistry students. There were too many lost causes around there, most of them victims of alcohol, the cheap and legal fix. I never unpacked my bag. Before the week's end, I was gone.

The garden was the only place left to go. It wouldn't be the first time I had slept on a lounge chair in the hallway.

\*    \*    \*    \*    \*    \*    \*

After working the indoor fields for five days, anxiety and paranoia became allies. I spent my days sleeping in the lounge chair in artificial darkness. At night, when the lights went on, I began to work. My body clock was so confused that I couldn't eat or sleep right. Combine that with no exercise, and you get a guy whose nerves are mush and whose brain could turn against him at any moment.

I'd only come out once in five days, for food and to make a few phone calls. When I got back to the warehouse, my old friends, anxiety and paranoia, welcomed me with open arms. I took a final look around outside. Two guys about a hundred yards down the street were stripping a parked car for parts. An old woman was walking aimlessly and directionless with her belongings in a carpetbag she carried on top of her head. And, of course, the omnipresent distant siren served to remind me of something Chet always said—"Just because I'm paranoid doesn't mean they're not watching me."

When the police bolt locked into place, the street sounds faded, only to be replaced by the sounds of fans, ballasts, pumps, and running water. As I opened the inside door, the intense glare stabbed at my eyes, sending me groping for my sunglasses. Even so, it took a while for my eyes to become accustomed to the twenty-two radiant globes that turned night into day.

Jim was supposed to have been there two days before. It sure would have been good to have someone to talk to. He was beating the bushes for seeds, and at last count, five thousand were all he could muster. Not enough to secure my future. Planting time approached, and I had promised the Midwesterners I'd deliver, and I would, if I had to grow them myself.

As I settled into my lounge chair early that morning, the unresolved questions in my head kept me awake. Where in the hell was I going to get sixty thousand seeds? Where and how was my lover? But mostly, when would I get out of that trap? And the answers to life's big questions continued to elude me. In fact, they were slipping further away. Who am I? What do I believe in? And what was over the horizon? The more I desired an answer, the harder it was to cope with the idea that there was no answer. I had become my garden, my lifestyle. My game was a fun one, but, like everyone else, I was trapped in it. This brief flash of awareness was not comforting. I am *not* what I do! I am *not* my job or my girlfriend's boyfriend! Who am I? I just am. A peaceful wave washed over me. Want and desire subsided. Escape from myself seemed possible. Sleep approached. With one final breath, I faded into dreamland.

＊　＊　＊　＊　＊　＊　＊

A warm wind gusting up the canyon from the ocean swept over me, blowing the thoughts from my mind. For precious moments, I felt the pressure release. Layers of unreality peeled off one by one. I could feel all the words that described me melting into the clouds that hovered just below at about three thousand feet. Stripped down to my essence, another reality came forth. The sun beat on me, but it felt as if the glow were coming from within. I wanted to share this moment of bliss, to somehow describe the indescribable. This was my reality. This was who I am. Words failed miserably when put to the task of defining me. Ironically, silence described who I am much better.

A four-pointed buck climbed out of the clouds cresting the adjacent ridge and saw me sitting not two hundred yards away. For a moment, we shared the sun and the wind. He was not afraid, nor did he seem surprised to see me this far out in the wilderness. The buck surveyed the area, then turned toward the cloud-covered ocean and lifted his face to the afternoon sun. The connection was undeniable. He "knew." Emotions welled up inside me. They cried for expression. A rhythm to be beaten on a drum. An abstract picture to be painted. A way to be. My eyes closed. I was full.

The air above my left ear ripped open, and before I could turn to look, the large bird was in front of me, careening down the canyon toward the sea. He circled a few times and landed on a sixty-foot, burnt, oak tree directly below me on the hill. Perched on a thick branch at the top of the tree just about eye level, the raven looked directly at me. He paused for a moment. I got the feeling I knew this bird. With a couple of squawks, he began to flap his wings and hop along the branch. His movements became more and more frenzied until he was out of control, but I felt I understood him. That crazy raven wasn't flapping and squawking. He was singing and dancing! I rose to my feet, laughing out loud and dancing along with the raven until I was exhausted. I felt consciousness slipping away... Then I awoke, and although I was still in the hallway lounge chair, I had a new perspective.

# CHAPTER 4

I remained in the chaise for almost an hour, reflecting on the last few years of my life. It was possible that I'd been doing things for the wrong reasons, reacting rather than acting. The axioms of the truth that never needed to be said had become mere slogans. Somewhere on Enlightenment Road I took a left turn at Desire Street, then a right on Want Way, and Want turned into Need, and sometime later I was looking for someone to draw me a map back to where I started.

That's who the raven was. That wasn't an escape dream. It was a message. A dream-o-gram: Time to come home. Stop. You're chasing your tail. Stop. Too much thinking can be dangerous. Stop. Signed, the Greedy Bird. And that bird was greedy too—for life. He wanted to squeeze it like a lemon, savoring every drop. Normally, I would rely on the Narrator for this kind of insight. He would calmly sit me down and then scream at me, "Look at you, you fool!" but I was so turned around that even the Narrator was a little dizzy.

"Down but not out," I heard him say from the area near my right shoulder.

"How do I find the path?" I uttered the words to an empty room.

"Close your eyes," the Narrator replied.

"How do I ask for direction?" I said.

"Without words," the Narrator replied.

"What voice will guide me?" I asked.

"Quiet," was his only response.

✳    ✳    ✳    ✳    ✳    ✳    ✳

The three clicks of the police bolt opening startled me, but I knew if it was a bust they wouldn't have a key. The brass knob on the inside door began to turn. It seemed like an eternity, but, as I had hoped, it was Jimmy's smiling face that crossed the threshold of our marijuana lab. I'd known Jim for twenty-nine of my thirty-one years, and other than getting bigger, he looked the same as when we were kids. The baby face was deceiving. A carefree grin, willing to cheerfully accept whatever came, did not portray the intricate workings of his mind.

We grew our first big garden together. The L & L. We were the two city boys of a three-man partnership. We moved up north in the summer of 1979 and lived in a Chevy van. The first Mobile Hilton. I would come down for a week here and there, but Jim would stay in the forest alone with the plants for weeks on end. That's where he got his nickname, Jungle Jim. In town, however, Jim was my hands. I thought of it, and he did it. If it was a logistics problem you had, JJ was your man.

Take this project, for instance. I explained to him that I had learned of a process for indoor growing that, at long last, would make an effort worthwhile. All I needed was a safe place and power, the two most difficult problems to overcome. His response was typical. "No problem. When do you want to get started?"

I had been pondering the power dilemma for a year. "How will you get power?" I asked, rather incredulously.

"We'll jump it," he answered, with equal nonchalance.

"Won't PG&E get hip to us?" The obvious question.

"I'll find out," he said.

"How?"

"I'll ask PG&E."

"Are you crazy?" I jumped.

"No, no, no," he said. "It's a snap. I'll approach some repairman with a good story and a crisp hundred-dollar bill, and he'll tell me whatever I want to know."

"How can you be so sure? Even if he goes for it, he'll probably just give you the company line—how you will get caught eventually and charged with grand theft electricity."

"What have I got to lose?" His lack of concern was disarming.

Having had no success passing on my angst, I tried another angle. "What about the building?"

"How big?" he replied, unshaken.

"A thousand square-feet would be a nice start," I said. "We don't want to buy a piece, so how will you deal with the landlord?"

"We could buy if we wanted to," he said. "Just put up a low down payment, pay the mortgage for as long as we need to, and then let the bank foreclose. Or, failing that, I speak perfect *landlordese*—triple rent."

I didn't see a flaw in his argument, even though the cavalier way he said it was unnerving. I knew he had the nuts to do it.

Almost two years later, he had successfully jumped all of my hurdles, and we were up and running. I knew he wouldn't be able to relate to my paranoia over being in the garden for a week straight. If I even tried to express it, I knew his response would be, "What's the problem, you wimp?"

"How you doing, bud?" he asked when he saw me resting in my makeshift bed. "Taking a nap?"

"No, I've been sleeping here all week."

"Gee, that could be tough on your nerves. How come?"

"Winston's place is an accident waiting to happen. I won't be staying there anymore."

"What about Charlie's house?"

"Charlie? She's dangerous!"

"Did you guys have a fight?"

"No, I wouldn't chance that. It seems Charlie had a run-in with the husband of one of the women down at the shelter. He must have pushed her a little too far. I read in the paper that his car was bombed, and I think she had something to do with it. No sign of police looking for her, but I split the hideout anyway."

"Where is she?"

"She's vacationing in sunny El Salvador!"

"Gee, those death squads are in for it," he said with a chuckle. "If they piss her off, she might overthrow the junta."

"Yeah, I can see it now. Generalisima Carlotta Mikos in khakis, smoking a big Cuban cigar and rallying the peasantry against the oppressor."

"Is there any word from her? Does she need any help?"

"Charlie? It's hardly likely. What about you? What did you find out about seeds? Are there any?"

"Yeah, I did very well for these times. I found twenty-thousand. Sixteen-thousand of one variety, a strong cross that looks really good. The buds they come from are very dense and pretty strong smoking. The grower made the seeds on purpose, so we know what the male plant is. I'm really happy with it. We still have to germinate them so we know what percentage will start."

"And the other four-thousand?"

"Well, as you might expect, they look okay, but I don't know what the hell they are. The guy says they are pure Indica, for whatever that's worth. No sample of the pot, and I don't even think he intended to have seeds, but they'll only cost you about forty-cents each. I guess you take what you can get."

"Okay. That sounds like a good start. Now about those other forty-thousand."

"That won't be easy," he said.

"Well, Walker has a good relationship with the Dutch. Maybe we can work out something with them."

"Wow, even you are reduced to paying the Seed Bank five bucks a seed." He said. "That's disgusting."

"I've changed my mind about those guys, though," I said. "I used to scoff at them when my seeds were plentiful and cheap and the strain was still good, but now they have to be the ones we look to, not only for good seeds, but also to keep the different varieties alive so we can still have them, should there ever be an opportunity to grow again outdoors. Not only that, but they can also isolate the qualities we like. Walker has been reluctantly using their seeds for three years, and now he says he just has to give in. They can try so many different combinations in eight-week cycles that we couldn't keep up with them outside in the best of conditions. They can breed for indoor, outdoor, and early harvest, not to mention the endless varieties of hybrids they can turn out. It's time we paid them the respect they're due."

"I don't mind paying them respect, but five dollars a seed is not respect, it's worship." He complained.

"Well, Walker is only paying three dollars for Big Haze, and he buys less than five-hundred a year. I think we can do better if we ask for tens of thousands."

"Like what?" he asked.

"Maybe two bucks, maybe one," I hoped.

"I liked it a lot better when we got the buck a seed. I feel like we've been replaced."

"Look at it this way," I said. "We were the biggest Indica seed sellers in the world. Now we're the biggest seed buyers. No one has ever bought thirty or forty thousand seeds from the Seed Bank. It's another first for us."

"Yeah, lots of glory, but when do we get paid?" he was inconsolable.

"Harvest time, buddy. These guys are planting *sixty* thousand seeds. We'll be the only game in town, and it will be on a very large scale."

"It feels like I've been waiting for the next harvest since high school," he moaned.

"Just think of how much fun you're going to have. You'll be running drivers and stash houses all over the place. This might be the biggest domestic sinsemilla project ever attempted. And we're very close. You'll be running my whole apparatus. Soon come, buddy. Soon come."

"Patience isn't my strong suit, but what else is new? How's about you? Don't you think it's about time you get out of here? I mean, get a life! You can't sleep in here forever. You have money. Get a place."

"Yeah, I've got to do something soon. I kind of lost my way. I think I need to backtrack, to get back in touch with where I want to go."

"Sounds very heavy," he said.

"Would you give me a break? I think I'll head up to Charlie's place for a few days to reconnoiter. Can you handle this for awhile?"

"Sure. I'll see you tonight. Is all the paperwork up to date here?" he asked, "so I can tell where we are?"

"Yeah," I assured him. "If you have any questions, I'm not going anywhere. You can ask me tonight."

"Okay, bud. Take off, 'ay!"

"Thanks," I said, hanging up my sunglasses and straightening out the work bench. "I'll see you later." As he bolted the doors behind me, I paused to soak up the sun and feel the cool breeze for the first time in days.

# CHAPTER 5

Beep! Hi, Charlie. If you get this, it's Angela. I hope everything is all right with you. Everything is peachy here. Tina is safe up north. The cops aren't interested in pursuing that other incident. What's-his-name hasn't showed his face anywhere near the shelter. We all love you, and we await your safe return."

"Beep! Hi, Charlie. Betty here. Just called to tell you that all is well in Legget. The work is all done, and the girls have gone home with their coffers full. We took down the shop and cleaned it spotless. I let them each take some of the stash you picked out for us. They were full of smiles, and so am I. When are we going to see you? Soon, I hope. Thanks for another great year. We love you."

"Beep! Jason? How you doing? This is Walker. It's been a long time. Call me."

"Beep! Hi, honey. It's mom. I know you're off on vacation, but I just wanted to remind you about your dad's birthday next month. He's turning fifty, you know, and we want to make a big to-do over it. The whole family will be there, and you will be missed if you don't come. We love you. Have fun. See you then. Beep! Beeeep!"

Just another typical set of Charlie's messages. She had her life turned up to ten. Time for everyone and time for no one, yet message after message, we love you, we love you, we love you. Didn't the girl have any bill collectors? The one message that was for me, however, was a good one. Walker—that was his real name, and it fit him perfectly—was the freest person I knew. Free of himself, mostly. He saw the unimportance of his own existence while bathing in the glory of it. One of the last true hippies, for lack of a better word. He had managed to reconcile the way he felt spiritually with the harsh, cold realities mom and dad always told us about. He was really just a regular guy who lived on a mountaintop with his wife and a crowd of beautiful, creative kids. The whole clan was a food-growing, music-making, artistic bunch, with Walker as the perfect example of letting out the "you" in you.

He was given to dancing at any time, and he liked to fly experimental kit planes that he made in the barn. That's why I called him "the Crazy Bird." I knew when I awoke from that dream that the crazy raven was Walker. And he was calling me, just as sure as if he had used Ma Bell herself. It was time to make the call. To play the no-game game for a while. Maybe share the mountaintop and a little silence with someone who could hear me when no words were spoken. But first I thought I'd get good and loaded well into the night and sleep until my eyes opened by themselves. For the first time in a long while, I had nothing to do, and sleeping until noon was the first activity of the day.

By the time Jim got to Charlie's house, Winston had already been and gone. He brought exactly what I wanted. Half a dozen Quaaludes would do the trick. They'd become almost impossible to acquire for two years, and it had been six months since my personal medicine chest had run empty. Half a 'lude and one glass of red wine later, we were pleasantly sedated, but the conversation remained lively. We could talk forever on just about any subject. Another half-Q and another glass of wine, and we had zeroed in on our favorite topic—not just growing pot, but revolutionizing the industry. We expected technology to continue to advance so fast, in so many new directions, that the police would always be one step behind. You see, the cops weren't stupid, they were just slow to act, and the pot grower was ready to take action. They say pot smokers lose their motivation, but you had to be a motivated beast to work that hard and take the risk of loss of crop and loss of freedom as well. Take my word for it, guerilla growing was not for the faint of heart. And growers had to be highly self-motivated. The trick was not to be stupid, to keep thinking ahead. So we'd gone indoors, but it wouldn't be long until they clamped down on that, too, although we figured with the rapid advance of indoor technology, in a few years consumers could conceivably grow their own.

Next we intended to explore the possibility of reclaiming the great garden sites of the past, lost to the pot cops, by laying carpets of two-ounce spikes late in the season. This was our pet project, and it was also our pet peeve.

*　　*　　*　　*　　*　　*　　*

You see, Jungle Jim and I were partners on the L & L project in 1979. We harvested the whole crop in one night, on a full moon, because the helicopter had practically landed on the site earlier in the day. It had come up the canyon and hovered right over garden number two at about five p.m., just about eye level with our campsite. We both watched from the bushes as the copter surveyed the area, but I guess they didn't have time that day, so they flew away. We stayed in the bushes until around ten p.m., but no one came. So we drove the truck right into all four gardens—something we hadn't thought possible—and harvested branches until three a.m., filling the bed of a side-boarded pick-up without any bags or boxes, of which we had none. Simply a tarp over the top and the spare tire to hold them down.

We used every dirt road in Mendocino County to avoid Highway 101, but eventually we had to come out, and we would still be in pot country. We made it most of the way to Ukiah before we hit the highway, and successfully delivered the crop to a safe place in the city. But that isn't the point. We left a few plants in the garden to see if the cops would bust it, and the plants matured for another two weeks before we harvested them. So we decided to try again the next year. Okay, sure, we took a few extra precautions. We made arrangements with a neighbor to keep our vehicles on his property, and we put in a lot less work, but we really didn't learn a thing. We planted big patches right in the same spots, right out in front of God and all His people.

Around about harvest time—in fact, September 3, 1980—we returned to the land at eleven at night, after spending the day with some friends who had a place on the Eel River. We never locked the gates because no lock ever kept a garden from getting busted, but there was no reason for them to be open. We parked off the property and made our way to the camp on footpaths. As we approached the first garden, we knew something wasn't right, but nothing prepared us for the total devastation we found in each plot. Fences mangled beyond repair, water lines axed into tiny pieces, and stumps where our girls used to be before they were hacked out by Big Brother and incinerated while still wet. The plants sizzled and screamed as they burned, but they still yielded their sacred smoke. The pot cops joked as the smoke billowed out of the incinerator at the local mill, which had been closed down until now. The unemployed mill workers had turned to growing, and now they saw their living going down in flames again, in the same mill. The final irony.

This after carrying manure on your back for miles in the hot sun, planting and tending your crop all summer, turning back the hunters, warding off the rip-offs, and hiding from the planes and helicopters that dropped combat troops into the woods with live ammo—troops that had been told there was an enemy in the woods ready to fight back. In California! Not Nicaragua! Then you returned home one day to devastation and a note that said, essentially, you're busted, and we're really gonna put your ass through the ringer now.

When we got to our campsite, all was quiet, but they had been there and torn the place apart. There wasn't anything left. No one got hurt or busted, but the memory lingered, and by the time the 'ludes were gone, Jim and I were pissed off all over again.

"Those fuckin' pigs," Jim snorted. "Who the fuck do they think they are?! We work our asses off all year long, and they rip it out without a care."

"Yeah, forget the spiritual or financial aspects of the thing. They didn't carry sacks of manure on each shoulder for hours until their ears were literally stuffed with shit," I complained, even though we had a good laugh at the picture that brought to mind.

"They didn't sleep on the rocks or deal with the bugs or the burrs in their socks or the heat or the dirt. They just came for the harvest," he said.

"It's a good gig if you can get it," I quipped.

"We need to find a way to fight back, blow up the helicopters or find some way to intercept them. Armed insurgency. We've got to organize. They've been pulling this shit too long." He was getting heated up.

"Take it easy, Jim. We'll beat them at their own game. This season, buddy, we'll regenerate all those old spots in pot country that have previously been busted, and we'll start with our own land. Yeah. You ready, man? Are you willing to move back into the woods and go for it?"

"Yeah, I'm ready!" he chimed right in. "I want to plant six hundred clones in garden three, wall to wall. And that's only the beginning. We'll franchise. If we set up a gigantic clone factory, we could supply hundreds of growers with females all year. No, thousands. We could just plant them in regular plugs. Ha! Easy. I could plant the whole flowerbed in front of city hall in an hour, then the rooftops. I wonder what the market is in Europe."

He was losing control, but who wanted to be the one to tell a rampaging lunatic hell-bent on evening the score to mellow out? "Hey, hey, Jim. It's okay, man. It's okay. Just sit down, man. We're going to do all that shit, but not tonight."

It was no use. He was on a roll, and there was no stopping him. I retired to the bedroom. Telling Jim to get some sleep, I closed the door behind me. As I lay there, I marveled at the comfort of a real bed. All the while, I could hear him in the next room talking to himself. "Organize... expand... we'll show those bastards!" I suppose he went on into the night. About fifteen minutes later, I passed out. It was the wonderful kind of comatose that only comes with all-out exhaustion but recharges your batteries for another full-tilt run.

# CHAPTER 6

I made it to Walker's just in time for the start of the harvest. He had three beautiful, fifty-plant patches about a hundred yards below the ridge road. These ladies had an awesome view of the California coast at its sheerest point, four thousand feet above Big Sur. They basked in desert sun a thousand feet over the cloud line. The spots were carved out of a twenty-foot-high wall of manzanita and madrone trees with hundred-year-old Monterey pines that towered overhead, threatening to drop their basketball-size cones. There was a deep thicket of underbrush and huckleberry that made passage impossible, except for a meandering, well-camouflaged rabbit trail that Walker had trodden to each spot. The C.A.M.P. helicopters flew up and down every crevice where there might be some water but never searched the area right around the dry ridge top. This meant a regular schedule of water deliveries, and, having helped out early in the summer when the plants were still small, I earned the honor of helping with the harvest.

Walker had a lookout with a palm-sized ham radio stationed on the ridge's highest peak. From this vantage, he had a bird's-eye view of the ridge road for a mile in each direction and would warn us in the unlikely event that we had company. I hiked into the gardens with Walker and was dumbfounded by what I saw. The once nicely separated plants, now ten feet tall, had completely filled the spaces between. Their enormous branches, laden with tops as long and fat as my leg, grew to touch each other, constructing a network of tunnel-like passages from which to work.

We harvested branches for about an hour, managing to cut the top half off a dozen of the extremely sticky Haze plants, and then carried them out on our backs in three trips apiece. It was a bushel of fun, but it wasn't easy work. I'd had my fill. Somebody else would have to harvest the other 144 plants. Walker saw my worn-out condition and promised to feed me well and treat me to a magical night. I agreed immediately. Who couldn't use a little magic?

\*     \*     \*     \*     \*     \*     \*

The family gathered for dinner around a large, circular, wooden table under the late-afternoon sun. Where the expansive sky above met the bed of clouds hovering below us, the curvature of the earth was plain, and above the sky, the brightest stars began to peak through the fading sunlight. I felt like a speck of sand on an impossible beach in a vast ocean.

We discussed the importance of our problems relative to time and space over a meal of rice and vegetables seasoned with psychedelic mushrooms. Then we set off on foot for the ridge and Miracle Valley beyond. Walker set a brisk pace for the first twenty minutes, as we climbed the last four hundred vertical feet to the ridge crest, a distance of a mile or so. From this lofty perch way above Big Sur, the coastline stretched out before us and the remote expanse of the Ventana Wilderness wrapped around our backs. By the time we reached the ridge trail, my heartbeat had quickened, and a slight euphoric feeling had come over me. We turned south along the ridge trail and as body and mind became more attuned to my present surroundings, time slipped away. A stiff, warm wind blew from the west, seemingly pushing us off the main trail onto a small fork. With the sun now completely set, the sky turned a glowing amber color. The trail came to a knoll overlooking a vast, prehistoric valley, virtually untouched by man. At that moment, a long-suppressed part of me broke through to consciousness. A familiar shiver danced along my spine, and a tear of joy reminded me that there was more to my existence than the harsh realities of my daily life.

We waited atop the overlook for a while, taking in the sunset as the wilderness darkened before us. I lit a joint of Elvis from the warehouse. The smoke expanded in my lungs, enhancing my awareness of the moment. My senses burned with the intake of information. Sights, sounds, and smells, normally only recorded and discarded, filled my experience. I passed the J to Walker. He looked into my eyes as he puffed. "Perfect," he said. "It's times like these that give you a real appreciation of what we do for a living."

"Yeah," I replied. After a while I tended to grow it and smoke it by rote, but from this high perspective, the reasons for planting and harvesting my crop became crystal clear once again.

The path narrowed as it descended into the valley, hidden from the casual traveler for centuries by 50,000 acres of wilderness to the east and the imposing Big Sur range to the west. I had to run to keep up with Walker, who always had one foot on the ground as he charged through the bush. My heart rate climbed again while I found my stride. With darkness creeping up on us, the forest moved in close. Walker stopped in a small area completely covered with tall bushes. He lit my last few footsteps with a small flashlight, allowing me to see him crouched on the path. As I knelt beside him, he turned out the light. "Listen," he said. At first I could only hear the thunder of my heart.

Then I heard something move in the brush behind us, a lizard perhaps. The wind washed over the bushes above my head and through the tall trees above them. I struggled to control my breath so that I could hear what he heard, and when I did hear it, I stopped breathing altogether to home in on the sound.

"Drums?" I said. How could it be, this far out into the wilderness? They were faint but unmistakable. "What are drums doing way out here?"

"They're calling you," he said. He turned the flashlight on himself. His eyes were glazed and his grin enormous, as if the cat were out of the bag.

He took off again. This time I was right behind him, putting my foot down where he picked his up, until we broke out of the bushes and the path was once again visible, this time by the light of the rising moon. The drums got louder. Flutes and other instruments became audible as we drew nearer. We ducked into the bush again for a short while. I began to see flickers of a campfire through the shrubs, and when we broke into the clearing, the air was filled with the overwhelming smell of burning sage. The modest fire was at the far end of a large meadow. Many people, at least twenty, were gathered in a circle of drums to the left of the fire. Their rhythm was slow and steady, as if waking. Children played in the meadow as we crossed. I began to make out tents and lean-tos in the woods around its edge. A flashlight pierced the doorway of the nearest tent, searched the meadow, and settled on Walker and me. A young woman popped out and bounded towards us. She gave Walker a big hug. "Hi," she said, "we missed you at sunset."

"We were on the knoll at the top of the trail," Walker said. "It was beautiful, wasn't it? This is Jason. Jase, this is Layla." She melted me with a gorgeous hug, then turned and bounced off toward the fire. I was hooked. We hadn't spoken, not even a hello. I couldn't even see her well, but I could feel that she was beautiful.

We approached the drum circle. I didn't see one familiar face, but the eyes were familiar. They all shared that glazed look of blissful acceptance. Many acknowledged my presence with a knowing glance. I looked back toward Walker, but he was gone. I fought the urge to follow him, stepped up to a conga drum, and joined in the hypnotic rhythm the group was beating out. Several of the drummers were excellent. I struggled somewhat to find a beat that would fit in. No one seemed to notice. Not all the drums were congas. Some made sounds that were new to me. And other instruments—flutes, a guitar, and a sax—wound through the rhythm. Outside the circle a group of revelers danced a kind of tribal stomp. All together, but each alone. One of them was Layla. Every part of her danced its own dance. Spontaneous creative movement. As the drums sped up, so did the dancers. Someone let out a howl, and other hoots and cries followed until the drums reached a fevered pitch and then stopped abruptly. The howling and cheering continued for a moment longer. The group then drifted apart for a while to rest.

I went over to the fire and sat down. Where was Walker? The thought came and went. I tried to follow it to the next rational thought, but the train of thoughts had been broken. I didn't know where I was, or for that matter, why, and it didn't seem to matter. I could feel. Blood rushed inside me. My eyes were filled with the shadow dance the firelight was doing in the trees.

Someone tapped my shoulder. It was Layla. She was holding a tall, plastic bottle of water. "Thirsty?" she asked, handing the bottle to me.

"Yeah, thanks," I said, taking a drink. "Just right."

She moved closer to the glow of the fire. I saw her clearly for the first time. She was stunning. Her long, thick, black hair matched incredibly with perfectly blue eyes. Her full-length skirt swirled back and forth as she drew patterns in the dirt with her toes. She stood about five-foot-three, with the thin waist of a young girl and the curves of a woman. She wore a loose top that came down to her midriff, leaving bare the area between her top and the wide waist-band of her skirt. I resisted the urge to cover that spot with my hands. My eyes rose from her belly to meet hers. She had caught me gazing at her body. I would have been embarrassed, if not for the look on her face. An innocent, yet totally inviting look. Not wanting to stare, I broke away from Layla's eyes and looked around the camp.

The drums began again. They settled on another slow beat. I glanced back at Layla to find her attention still fixed on me. I searched for words, as the quiet between us was deafening. "Uh, how often do you come here?" I asked.

She sat down beside me and spoke softly, as if the words might disturb us. "I've lived here for five months," she answered. "Is this the first time you've come down into the valley?"

"Yeah. When Walker said we were going for a hike, I had no idea what was in store. You've stayed in the woods for five months?" I had thought two weeks alone with my summer patch was a lot. "Are you hiding?"

"No, there is no hiding," she said. "When I first came to Miracle Valley I was kind of running away from my troubles, but there's no easy escape."

"It can't be easy, living in a tent out in the middle of nowhere for five months," I said.

"It isn't," she replied. "In fact, it's quite difficult, and I am still going to have to deal with what I was running away from."

"Then why do it?" I asked. The thoughts were coming out more easily now and in some kind of rational order as the effect of the mushrooms temporarily waned.

"Why?" she repeated incredulously. "How, who, when... I don't even ask. The questions have no meaning to me. They beg for righteous answers where there is no answer. Where do I come from? Where am I going? Why do I exist? I could chase the why forever."

"Then what guides you?" I asked.

"I just do," she said. "No answer is the answer. I take comfort in that."

The drums had picked up, and there was a lot more activity around the camp. Layla stood up in front of me and began swaying in time to the beat.

"If you don't pursue the reasons for living, what's left?" I felt like a babe in the woods compared to this young woman, wise beyond her years.

She reached out to me with both hands and pulled me to my feet. We stood close enough to embrace. "Living," she said. "Right now." Another question was pursed on my lips. She rose to her tiptoes and kissed it away. "Don't ask," she said, "just celebrate." With that, she pulled me out to where the tribe was dancing—thirty or forty of us now—dancing around each other like children full of wonder, weaving a pattern of life far beyond thought.

The drums pounded in my head as my bare feet pounded the dirt. It took twenty minutes for me to get my second wind, twenty minutes of aerobic exercise, but then the mushrooms wound back up and took over. The dancers had worked a deep soft spot in the ground where we danced. The soil was crushed into fine powder, and my toes were buried in it. We danced freely in and around one another, somehow managing to keep from bumping into each other as our arms and legs flailed about. Walker had joined the drum circle, and they began to really cook.

My body was moving in ways of its own design. Hands, arms, hips, all seeming to know where they were going without my having to think about it. I marveled in their creativity, as if detached and observing from a third person's perspective. Faster still, the drums drove me out of myself. Peaking on mushrooms and out of breath, but unwilling to stop or even slow down, with dozens of people around me in the exact same place.

We shared that moment as if all were one. No words passed, but we were closer than Funk is to Wagnall. Finally the drums climaxed, and everyone let out whatever sounds were inside them. The howling lasted a long while after the beat was gone. Four or five people were in a group hug. I caught Layla's eyes, and a big smile broke onto her face. We both joined the hug at once. Ten, then twenty, then thirty. The hug got bigger, all caressing and singing some inner tone.

Layla and I continued to hug long after the rest of the group had drifted apart, hugging and humming until we both began to laugh at the same time. She took my hand and started off through the meadow to her tent. As we passed the fire, she tossed a large handful of sage onto it, causing a plume of sweet-smelling smoke to rise into the air.

She was well provisioned. The floor was completely covered with one big bed and a large, thick quilt. Her clothes were stacked neatly to one side, leaving plenty of room for us to spread out. She lit a hanging candle, and we shared the last of her water. Then she turned her attention to me. She approached with the look of a hungry animal. Her first kiss was almost a bite. With both arms wrapped around my head, she kissed my face again and again, stopping every so often to feed on my lips. Her hands searched my body as if I were being frisked. When she found the button to my pants, she ripped it open, pushed me backwards, and pounced on me before my back hit the bed. I tried to caress her in a loving manner. Lightly touching her face, then neck, I explored her body, stopping to draw tiny circles just below the waistband of her skirt, but she had no patience for that. It only seemed to inflame her. We took off our clothes, and I lay back while she poured over me. She teased me with her lips and tongue until she had me right where she wanted me, then climbed on top and ground her pelvis into mine. There was little romance about it. This was an attack. Her hands caressed first my chest and then her own, as she raised and lowered herself faster. It took about three minutes for her to climax, and then, with a sigh, she kissed me once more and curled up next to me. I kissed her face and eyes while she caught her breath. She snuggled in close as if ready for sleep. My kisses trailed down her front until my lips hovered over her fur. The instant my tongue touched her, she came alive again. Barely touching her, I teased and tickled for what seemed like an eternity, pausing every so often to reach deep inside her. Each time she tensed up, I would stop, causing her to claw at the bed as if she were trying to get away, but we both knew she wasn't going anywhere.

I drew myself up to her face and kissed her. A different kind of kiss. The long, soft kind that lasts for days. I teased and tickled the tip of her upper lip just as I had done below as I slowly eased into her. She let out a deep, guttural sound and searched my mouth with her tongue. We made love as slowly as possible. I put myself in low gear and left it there. When she seemed anxious, I would speed up, only to quickly return to a crawl, until waves of delight washed over us both at once.

It lasted a long time. We squeezed each other until the spasms were gone, then we rolled around playfully for a few minutes, hugging as if trying to get inside one another. After awhile we curled up in the quilt and drifted off to sleep. Not the comatose sleep that I was used to, but a warmer and more secure kind that comes with having someone you love right next to you.

When my eyes opened, I found Layla staring into them. We were still in the same position. Outside, the blue jays were stirring up quite a ruckus. I could smell food cooking, and I was very hungry, but I didn't want to leave the flower in my arms. We made love again, like lovers who have known each other forever. When we opened the flap of the tent, the morning sunlight streamed in. The trees across the meadow were alive with color. Trees I had taken for granted for so long looked new to me, as if I could see past the definition into the being of them.

I found Walker standing at the campfire. "There's plenty of food if you're hungry," he said with that Cheshire-cat grin on his face. "How you doin'?"

"I don't think I could be doing any better," I answered.

"You about ready to hike out of here?" he asked. "I ought to get back to the house."

I looked around—the meadow, the campfire, the woods, the place where the drum circle had been and where the heroes had danced. I took a deep breath. "Let's wait awhile," I said. "Let me get my bearings."

I returned to the tent with two cups of tea and shared my last hour with Layla. "Will I see you again?" I asked hopefully.

She nestled into my lap. "I'm sure our paths will cross again," she said. "I'll be in the valley till the rains come and the trimming's done. After that, Walker will be able to find me."

"I'll come looking for you," I said. "I need more of this."

We kissed until Walker appeared in the doorway. "Hey, honey, how ya doin'?" he asked.

She stayed curled up in my lap and reached out for Walker's hand. "Ummm," she moaned in response.

"We're going to hike out of the valley," he said. "Do you want to come along?"

She thought for a moment. "No, I think I'll stay in this nice warm bed. I'll see you the next time you come down." She had one of those long, deep hugs for each of us, and then, with a quick good-bye to the rest of those gathered, we headed back the way we had come.

When we reached the knoll at the top of the trail, we turned back for a last look at Miracle Valley. A tear welled up in Walker's eye. He smiled at me. No words were spoken. He put his arm around my shoulder as we walked back to the ridge trail. It was hot now, as we faced into the sun and headed back into the real world.

# CHAPTER 7

If jumping the electrical didn't kill you and the cost of setup didn't bury you, all it took were about five-hundred man-hours to build one of those airtight, light-tight, soundproof, urban-guerilla gardens. My new partner and I had been pouring money and time into my second garden for four months. It could have honestly been done cheaper and faster, but we wanted this garden to last for a long time, so we made an extra effort. This time we set up in a suburban, upper-middle-class neighborhood under his three-story house in the hills with a swimming pool and all the amenities. Unlike the warehouse garden, the paranoia factor would be almost nil. I'd be able to relax. I could be in this garden eight hours a day, if necessary, without going berserk. After hijacking the power and installing our own hidden 200-amp electrical panel, we had to put in the floor, double all the walls, and insulate, then add a high-powered ventilation system and all of the electrical and plumbing from scratch. But finally the sinks and tanks and outlets were all in, and the only thing remaining was to hang the lights and bring in some cuttings from the warehouse.

On my way back to town from Walker's, I purchased the sixteen lights we would need. When the timers kicked over and the lights came on for the first time, my partner's face lit up as well. His is a common story. Drake Stewart was one of those who came to San Francisco when the song called, a guy with an open heart looking for a way to escape the suit-and-tie existence that his parents had lovingly prepared for him. After a few years in California, he had established quite a heavy pot business. In the early seventies, Columbian pot was all the rage, and rightfully so. It was the smoker's choice—fresh, gold, and exotic. American entrepreneurs were just beginning to ship huge, multi-ton boatloads into East Coast ports, and Drake was well connected back east. In no time, he was moving thousand-pound loads weekly. But by 1980, when Congress turned the navy loose on smugglers outside territorial waters, the lucrative Columbian pot business ceased to exist. Drake had amassed around half-a-million dollars, and, like thousands of other Columbian dealers, he had become quite comfortable sucking on the Columbian tit. By '82, with hundreds of tons of weed rotting on the docks of Cartagena and Santa Marta, the Columbians converted their marijuana fields to *coca*, a product that could be smuggled more easily, and by giving massive credit lines, they were able to convert their entire marijuana distribution network to cocaine. They could get a gram of coke into a consumer's hot little hands faster than Sears could get to Roebuck. All through the 80s, Drake risked everything in the coke trade. It wasn't a safe way to make a living. Those who didn't blow it by consuming their stock risked being ripped off by unsavory characters, getting busted by hoards of new D.E.A. agents, or even getting killed. These things were very rare in the pot trade, especially if you sold domestic hemp.

By the late 80s, the price of cocaine had dropped to $500 per ounce. There was so much that the supply had way outstripped the demand, and it became almost impossible to make a living. Finding himself in the position of taking all the risk with so little profit, Drake wanted to quit, but with his funds dwindling, he didn't know how he would pay the mortgage, and, at forty-five, he wasn't about to go out and get a job. So with my help, he found a way to have the house earn enough to make the monthly payment and support him in the style to which he had become accustomed. But the reason he was so happy wasn't the money. He felt he had come full circle. He had survived the coke years, and now he was back in the business he loved. He'd be producing the buds he sold, literally homegrown. And for true believers, that was a righteous place to be.

Two short days after receiving the lights, the garden was intact. The entire system was operational before we brought in a single cutting. Jungle Jim had been doing his job well at the warehouse. He was able to give me enough beefed-up clones to plant ten in my mother's room to take cuttings from later, plus two hundred fifty more to fill half my bloom room. Garden number two lurched into production. For the next six weeks, we took cuttings to fill first the clone box, then the beefing section, and, finally, the rest of the bloom room. By the time the whole room was filled, the first half was ready to harvest. It had taken Drake and me about thirty hours apiece each week to keep the room in top shape and to get him up to speed on the process enough for me to take a breather.

*　*　*　*　*　*　*

As I drove away from Drake's after a long day in the garden, a white Ford sedan pulled out from behind a parked truck about four houses away. I could tell he was tailing me, but before I could react, there was a red light flashing from the Ford's dashboard. Before pulling over, I lit my emergency cigarette to mask the overwhelming smell of freshly harvested mota in the trunk. I don't smoke, but I kept this stale cigarette in my glove box for months for just such an occasion. The buds were triple-wrapped in heavy garbage bags, but that did virtually nothing to stop the odor. In my side view mirror, the blue suit was already getting closer. With no time to exit the car, I started to puff harder on the cigarette. As I rolled down the window, the smoke bellowed out. The tobacco was beginning to make me nauseous. "Is there something wrong, officer?" I asked.

"Yes, sir. May I see your driver's license and registration, please... pal," he answered.

I jerked my head around to see the smirk on Chester Hawthorne's face. "You son of a bitch! You scared the shit out of me!"

"What's the matter? Is that some kind of contraband I smell, or did you just run over a skunk?" he said.

"How did you find this place, and what kind of cockamamie outfit is that?" I asked, still in shock. He was wearing a security uniform and hat with some kind of phony badge on the pocket. He looked the part, right down to the patent-leather shoes. He even had a utility belt and, of course, a gun in holster.

"I followed you here from your place. This is my police disguise. Do you like it?" he said, modeling.

"Yeah, sure, but not in my rearview mirror," I complained.

It had been months since I had delivered the sixty-thousand seeds to Chet at the merry-go-round in Berkeley's Tilden Park. Afghan Dan had come up with ten-thousand, and Walker squeezed thirty-thousand out of the Dutch for a reasonable price. I'm sure it was the biggest sale they had ever made. Chet was nowhere to be found all summer, and now he was back with good news. We talked right there in the street for about five minutes. "Hair; brown. Eyes; brown," he pretended to write me a traffic ticket while he gave me the numbers. Ten-thousand females grown in full sunlight. They were small, but he said to expect a final harvest of over four-thousand pounds. We could then expect to have access to just about one-third or less, depending on how fast we could move it. Ten days until harvest and twenty more to get it to me.

"So that gives you four weeks to get everything ready," he said, "and I want this done right." He gave me a list of things to arrange and then handed me his ticket book and pen. "Sign on line twenty-four, sir, please," he said.

I laughed. "Right. This isn't an admission of guilt, is it officer?"

"No, just a promise to appear," he said, as he tore off the ticket. Looking me right in the eye, he smiled and handed it to me. "Have a nice day, sir." He returned to his unmarked LTD and sped off.

"Thanks, officer," I said loudly as he pulled away.

It had been two seasons since the Midwesterners had grown a crop, but for the five years previous to that, they consistently grew more pot each year than every grower I knew combined. In that time, they had planted over two-hundred-thousand seeds, and each time, their buds were the sunburnt, sugar-glazed, chunky variety that we all loved so much. Even with outdoor growers forced to grow smaller crops in the shade, somehow these guys produced nearly a thousand pounds of A-grade stash each year. Sealed in double plastic bags and delivered to our door in case boxes of twenty-four, on credit. They were a serious throwback to the old days. Then the question became how to secure twelve to thirteen hundred pounds of the three-thousand-a-pound buds and then safely distribute it.

JJ and I went right to work. We found a huge, fancy house in Kensington with a three-car garage with electric doors and moved him into it. Jim built a hidden room behind a false cinderblock wall under the house. It was big enough for a family to hide in when the Nazis came. It took him two weeks, but when it was finished, it was impenetrable. When Chet saw it, he was thoroughly impressed. He began delivering boxes within days. The first van pulled into our garage with thirteen cases of the green gold, approximately $900,000-worth of weed. It was more than I had ever seen, let alone been responsible for, but since our benefactors were willing to undercut the market, it wouldn't be difficult to sell. Between the three of us, we dumped seventy pounds the first week. No one else had any buds out there, and we knew that would mean a good, long season for us. Before long, we had cars delivering buds to heads all over the country. It was too easy. Chet was in his glory. All his wheels were turning. The pay phones were humming, and the meeting places were busy. As soon as we cleaned out one load, another would arrive. No sooner had that truck gone, than another came. Drivers I had never met from parts unknown arrived at the door with a password and a bag full of cash, and left before the next truck pulled in. Jim and I flew into places like LA, Seattle and Denver to meet with long-time friends who would order thirty pounds or so—$100,000-worth of weed—on the strength of a one-ounce sample. We had a huge supply of quality stash in the middle of an all-time seller's market. Over the winter months the three of us sold about two-hundred pounds a week, more than two thousand. Double what we had hoped to do. Chet and I split $200 a pound, and Jim and I split that $100 down the middle. A $100,000 season would get all of my debts squared away and keep me comfortable for another year. Jim decided to take some time off, but I knew he would go through that money like a buzz saw and be back in the garden before summer. I could handle it until then. In fact, I needed a place to continue the apprenticeship of my new partner. He had been voraciously reading all the back issues of *High Times* and *Sinsemilla Tips* that he could find, but he'd learn more about how to grow in a few months of hands-on practice in my huge garden than he could ever learn in print. I also managed to bring Chet into the warehouse garden. He was blown away by what he called a "great achievement" and wanted to know everything that I knew on the spot. By mid-January, Chet was gone again. In a phone call with Jim, he left his final instructions on where to drop the last payment and what to do with the leftovers. Close to twenty pounds had spoiled or turned to shake. We dropped the price over and over until it became obvious that they weren't worth more than a couple of hundred dollars each. When I got to the stash house, Jim had the whole place packed up, and he was ready to move out. Several boxes were already in my van, and the house was virtually empty except for a twenty-pound pile of weed in the middle of the living room floor. The house thermostat was turned up to ninety, and Jungle Jim was sitting shirtless on an overturned milk crate in front of the pile, stuffing it into one-gallon Ziplocs at a ferocious speed.

"What the fuck are you doing?" I asked.

He looked at me with a stoned, boyish smile and said, "I'm quick-drying the stuff."

"What for?"

"Chet called and told me to, quote, 'distribute' it at whatever price you can get.'"

"So do you have a buyer or something?" I asked.

"Or something," he replied.

"What do you mean by that?" I began to worry. "Why are you putting it in quarter-pound bags?"

"Well, you see, here's my idea. Now hear me out, okay? These guys sold over ten million dollars in weed, right?"

"Well over," I agreed.

"Right, so they don't need or want this crap. And it's just a big risk for us to sit on this worthless shit, right?"

"True, a big risk for no gain."

"Right, and I know how you hate that, so I just figured that I'd bag it up and distribute it to the street."

"To whom," I asked, not sure if I wanted to hear the answer.

"Well, to the street, literally," he gleamed.

"Huh?"

"I'm going to drive around Berkeley and throw it out of the car window to people—on the street," he said triumphantly.

"What?" I yelled.

"Yeah, think about it. We can't sell it, but at least someone can get high. I was thinking about all those people down in People's Park. Some of them might be able to get a room for a couple of nights."

I paused for too long.

"What do you think?" he asked.

"I think you're out of your fucking gourd," I said. "Just think about it, driving down Telegraph Avenue tossing bags of weed out at all those unsuspecting onlookers?"

"Sounds like big fun to me," he laughed.

We kicked back on the sun deck and reminisced on what a good season we'd had. We smoked a few joints, and Jim got out his stash 'ludes, my favorite. By dark, he had me and all that weed loaded into the van so we could drive around town "distributing" it. When we got to Telegraph, the streets were lined with people—students, freaks, and homeless alike—milling around the coffee houses and pizza parlors. Until then, Jim would throw out a bag here and there to some deserving stranger, but now he looked at me with a crazed grin on his face. He jumped into the back, opened the side doors, and began to fling the weed out indiscriminately. Froth started to gather at the corners of his mouth, and I began to get a little worried, so I sped up. Jim's furious arms nearly carried him out the door. By the time we got out of the neighborhood, he was lying on the bed in the back, winded and laughing, charged with pride and reveling in glory.

# CHAPTER 8

It was five o'clock in the afternoon, and I was in the new garden when my beeper went off. I hated beepers, but this one was necessary. The only messages I got on it were regarding the warehouse garden. We set up some signals for protection. Each time I went into the room, I checked the beeper's status. The number 888 on the beeper meant the person tending could use some help when I got a chance. The number 505, or "SOS," meant, "need help right away," and three sixes meant, "stay away—police." We paid a guy in the building across the street to keep one eye out the window and one hand on the phone. Lately I had been getting a lot of wrong numbers paging me, but this time the signal was 505. Jim needed help right away.

I finished what I was doing in my hilltop patch and headed down to the war zone, where the only thing that flourished was my warehouse crammed to the rafters with green bud. As usual, I parked my van two blocks away and walked the rest of the way in. Jungle Jim was taking a break when I got there. He was sitting on the floor in the bloom room with his back up against the wall. Scattered all around him were large piles of leaf. A tiny hash pipe hung from his lip as he scraped a razor blade across resin-covered fingertips. He was in the middle of a ten-day period where two-thirds of our bloom room would be ready at once—close to twenty pounds—and with Charlie still out of town, we would be trimming it ourselves. When I saw Jim there in all his glory, I had to laugh. He looked up at me through glassy eyes, squinting from the glare of the lights. I could tell he was really frosted.

"Hey, man, check this out." He held up a ball of sticky Elvis finger-hash the size of a ping-pong ball. "Look how much I've got, and it's really strong, too."

"I can tell by those puffy eyes and the grin on your face," I said. "How long did it take you to collect that?"

"This is just from yesterday. There was a bunch more, but I had to test it out."

"Yeah, it looks like you tested it out... in, up, and down. It's no wonder you're sitting. How is it going here?" I asked after he exhaled.

"Well, everything is going great, but if I don't get some help soon, I'll be behind on the harvesting and trimming. That in turn will prevent me from planting the new stuff on time, which will delay the next harvest."

"How far have you gotten?" I asked.

"I've cut and trimmed three lights, but there are still nine lights to go. For some reason, they're all coming out together, and the other six lights will be ready in two weeks. Look at these babies!" he said proudly. We examined the whole room together. For the first time in two years, we had the entire building filled and each light producing up to its potential. The whole place was spotless. The mother plants were dark green and healthy, without any dead leaves or bugs on them.

"You're really doing a great job, Jim. The building has never looked so good."

"Thanks, man." The excitement bubbled in his voice. "How much do you think it is?"

"It's over sixty grand for sure," I said.

"Oh, can you believe it? Sixty-K at once. That's like an outdoor harvest. What are we going to buy? Where are we going to go? Let's have a party! Yeah, a huge party... on some Caribbean island! Just you and me and twenty of our best friends. We'll bathe in champagne and have massive orgies with beautiful island girls, tanned to perfection. How much do you think that would cost?"

"I think you are getting a little carried away. Maybe we could build another garden with that money."

"Always the voice of reason," he complained. "Let's go out and blow the whole wad. Easy come, easy go. We'll be kings for a month or so, and then we'll be able to go back to work."

"Okay, we'll do it!" I said

"Really? The whole wad? No matter what it takes?"

"Yeah, we'll piss away the whole thing. It's about time we let off a little steam." I could see he was getting wound up again, and I certainly wasn't going to be the killjoy in his moment of splendor.

"All right! We'll go absolutely nuclear!" he said. "We'll be radioactive for weeks on end. We haven't really partied together since the L & L. It's been all work and worries, but now we're going to blast off. How long do you think it will take to harvest and trim the rest of this?"

"About six man-hours a light. Do we have enough beefed-up clones to plant all twelve lights?"

"More than enough," he answered quickly.

"And then there are all the newly rooted clones that have to be moved into the beefing section, and we'll have to take enough cuttings to fill up the clone box again. About eight or nine days."

"Oh, shit! And we'll still have to go sell it." His shoulders slowly lowered as if the air had been let out of them. Then the familiar look of determination to forge ahead until the job was done returned to his face as reality poked up its ugly head. "All right," he said. "Let's get to it." He sat back down where I'd found him, amongst the piles of leaf. In a flash, the contented grin and glassy eyes returned. "But first you have to try some of this stuff I cut off my fingers." He tore off a hunk of sticky hash, and we smoked it before going to work.

Over the next few days, we established a work pattern that got the job done. JJ harvested and trimmed, while I replanted the bloom lights and the beefing section. When we finished that, we both took more cuttings to put in the clone box to root. On the third afternoon, about halfway through the fourth light, Jim called to me from the bloom room. "Jason, your beeper's going off."

"Can you shut that damn thing off? It's been driving me crazy," I said through the mother-room door, but when I looked up, Jim was standing in the doorway, his face ash white, his mouth open in shock. In his hand was the beeper, and he was holding it up so I could see the numbers... 666.

\*     \*     \*     \*     \*     \*     \*

I thought my body would seize up from the onrush of chemicals released by my natural sense of danger. First, the problem of a possible police raid, compounded by an almost debilitating adrenalin rush. We both looked toward the hiding place in the wall behind the kitchen sink and then at each other. Through the peephole in the front door, I saw one lone cop car out front. Trapped! The hiding spot was under the floor of the warehouse next door, only twenty inches high but wide enough to lie down in. We had placed cushions and some food in there, but we never really believed it would fool anybody. I sprang over to the cupboard under the sink and removed a screw in the back wall that opened a panel just large enough to shimmy through. Jim handed me a flashlight.

"Okay, come on in," I said.

"Bullshit," he said, disappearing from view. "Let's at least get what's cut down."

"Get your ass in here, you fool!"

He appeared at the sink again. "Here, take this!" he said, stuffing five garbage bags through the hole.

"Are you out of your mind? Get in here!"

"Take 'em, and I will!"

I shoved the bags behind me. "All right, now come on!"

He squatted at the sink and then stopped to listen. "I can cut the rest of it."

"No, Jim, goddammit! It isn't worth it!" There was no stopping him. I could hear him hacking down plants wholesale and stuffing them into plastic. I poked my head back into the room just as he tossed a full bag at the hole.

"Here, take this," he yelled. I crawled out of the hole to retrieve the bag and stuffed it inside. Jim had already filled another two bags with wet plant and was starting to wail through the remaining six lights of immature plants.

"Leave those! They aren't even ready!" I yelled as I dove back into the hole.

"They're as ready as they'll ever be," he said calmly, as he was furiously hacking away.

I heard several more cars screeching to a halt outside. "They're here!" I screamed in a whisper.

Jim was still working when they started pounding on the back door. He stuffed the last worthwhile plant into a bag and ran toward me. I moved back into the spot. The police bolt lasted long enough for him to jam in the last bag, crawl in behind it, and close the cupboard door. As the back door came crashing down, Jim was carefully replacing the cleansers and chemicals under the sink. Then he closed the inside panel, and we lay scrunched up with twelve bags of wet bud, in pitch darkness, trying not to breath. Jim was giggling under his breath, a kid hiding from his parents.

"What are you laughing about?!" I whispered.

"I got it all!" he said, like a crazed madman.

"You fucking idiot."

\*     \*     \*     \*     \*     \*     \*

We stayed in that position, barely moving, for more than four hours, listening to the police pillage the place. They destroyed twenty full-grown mother plants, about 350 beefed-up clones, and everything in the clone box. They dusted for fingerprints, took pictures, and confiscated our scales, our calendar, our bathroom towels, and some other stuff. They paid special attention to the electrical jump in the attic, but they scared us to cold stone when they found the chemicals under the sink. They spent a lot of time recording the labels of each bottle. One sneeze—one giggle—and we would have been undone.

Around nightfall, they sealed the place up, put up some police tape, and went away. They left all the equipment, so we assumed they would be back the next day to get it. We waited awhile before quietly reentering the room. We were alone, but through the eye piece on the front door, we saw a police car still parked across the street. We waited forty minutes for him to leave, but every time one left, another one arrived within a few minutes.

After two more hours, a police van pulled up to the front door, and five guys jumped out. This time, Jim was the first one in the hole. We scurried about twenty feet under the adjoining warehouse, dragging the twelve bags of Elvis buds with us. This crew really tore the place apart. They ripped out all the lights, pumps, fans, timers, tanks, buckets, trays, and tables and threw them into the van like so much garbage. We continued to slide backwards farther under our neighbor's floor until I felt something long and sharp knife into my lower back on the right side. I let out a muffled yell. Jim shone the light on me and eased me forward off a piece of steel that was sticking out of the floor joist.

"Aw, shit!" I cried out a little too loudly. "How bad is it?" I asked, knowing it was bad.

"You've been stuck like a bloody pig," he said, "but you'll make it."

Just then we heard several loud thuds. We thought they had heard me scream and were trying to break through the false panel in front of us, but when we heard the thuds again, they were clearly at our rear, away from the garden. A few more good thuds, and a hole opened up where the plaster wall met the foundation. Fresh oxygen streamed in to replace the dank air we had been breathing for hours. Then a flashlight poked into the hole and shined right on us. Busted!

Then, just when I thought it was all over, I heard a warm voice whisper, "I knew you would be in there."

Jim started to giggle again. "It's Charlie!" he said.

"No shit?" I couldn't believe it.

"No shit," Charlie repeated. "Now, you want to get the hell out of there?" A few more thuds, and Charlie had the hole opened wide. We scurried to it. She had the Mobile Hilton parked in the alley, one warehouse away from our busted garden. She had simply stopped the van there, got out, and smashed a hole in the wall with a fifteen-pound sledgehammer. When I poked my head through the newly crafted hole, she was standing right there with her precision tool in hand. When she saw I was hurt, she dropped it and helped me through the hole and into the van.

"Charlie, take this," Jim whispered through the hole.

Charlie went back. "What's this," she asked

"Buds," he said.

She took the bag and threw it into the back. "Oh, my god," she gasped.

"And more buds, and more buds, and more buds," answered the marijuana monster who lived in the hole under the garden, as bag after bag popped through the hole.

"Good for you guys," Carlotta said, loading them into the van and closing the side door behind her. Jim climbed in behind the wheel. Charlie ripped off my tee-shirt and used it to apply pressure to the wound. "How long ago did this happen?" she asked.

"Just a few minutes ago," I said.

"Good. Hold onto this and apply pressure." She went forward and knelt behind the driver's seat so she could see. "Okay, go nice and slow into the street right out in front of them. Slowly!"

"We beat those bastards this time," Jim giggled.

"Shut up!" snapped Charlie. "Pay attention!"

Jim drove right past the cops and the workmen like we were invisible. "We got you, you fuckin' pigs," he snorted, starting to get a little wild. He picked up speed, a little too much speed, as we pulled away. But unlike me, Charlie doesn't stand for foolishness. She popped him one on the right side of his head.

"Slow this fucking thing down and straighten up, you little prick!" Jim thought that was even funnier, but he did slow down

# CHAPTER 9

Once on the freeway, we began to wonder just how much the cops knew. If they had been watching us long enough, they might have known where the other garden was. That would have been another crushing blow. I'd always assumed that if I got busted in one garden, the other would pay my bail. We decided the hideout had to be safe. Neither Jim nor I had been there for over a week, and the call Charlie received from our lookout was the first one she had received since returning from El Salvador.

On the way, we stopped at a phone booth to call my partner, Drake, in the other garden to see if all was okay. Everything was all right, but we decided that since three-fourths of the garden was within a week of harvest, we should get it all out right away and at least clean out all the contraband before the storm troops arrived.

When we dropped Jim off at the hideout, Carlotta picked up some things that we would need for our escape. Jim was somewhere between being elated over finally beating our archenemy—the pot police—to the punch and being pissed off at me for trying to stop him instead of helping. I didn't really consider the loss of our garden a victory, although bagging the results with the wolf at the door was a triumph.

"We finally snookered those assholes this time," he jeered, "and you with your incessant conservatism. Jesus, man, control yourself. You'd think the world was coming to an end the way you skidded into that hole like a mouse from a cat. If I had listened to you, we would have got diddly. Instead, we beat the bust, made off with the goods, and left the bobbies holding their nightsticks. I'd just love to have seen the looks on their faces when they realized it had been ripped out just before they arrived. You know, that humid, acrid smell that takes over the room when you harvest?"

"Yeah, even with just one light, never mind all of them. It must have been obvious to them," I chimed in.

"You guys got all eighteen lights?" Charlie asked.

"Not 'you guys,'" Jim said. "Me."

"He stayed in the room cutting down plants until literally the last second," I replied. "You bozo!"

"Yeah, sure, I may be a bozo, but the fact remains we have a dozen bags of wet plant here, and even better than that, not one bud for the awful sirs."

I wanted to leave the crop with Jungle Jim at the hideout and go to the hospital, but Charlie said she would take care of me and the weed, if that was okay with Jim, and it was. When we left, he was in the best head space I'd ever seen him. Bursting with pride over his big win, one which he considered long-overdue retribution for the plunder of our last L & L garden. With pockets full of money left over from the winter and the prospects of twenty-five pounds hanging, he seemed not to fear reprisals over the warehouse seizure. He was set to kick up his heels at the hideout and wait for payday.

I gave Charlie directions to my other garden. None of my friends had ever been there. She was impressed with how together it was compared to the warehouse. In one-third the amount of floor space, there were almost as many lights, leaving no space unused. Everything was in its place, secured, labeled, and cleaned. She stroked me well for my accomplishment, knowing that due to the clandestine nature of my work, no one but Drake ever had before.

Drake's wife insisted on properly cleaning and bandaging my wound, while he and my heroine picked yet another crop before the gendarmes could. They packed the buds and all of the contraband garbage, like rock wool, wet leaf, and other incriminating things, into the van. There was no place to put them, so they had to cut down the last known Elvis moms. Then they burned all the dry leaf and paperwork, hosed the whole room down, and cleaned it spotlessly. The next day Drake packed all the gear into a truck and stored it in a rental unit, but for the moment all the equipment remained set up but shut down, another unhappy discovery should the police come.

We left Drake to go over the rest of his house with a toothbrush and headed across the bay and up Highway 101. Charlie filled me in on her trip to Central America along the way. She said it wasn't much fun. She successfully delivered the guns, but the romance went out of it when she was accosted by a gang of heavily armed youth that turned out to be a death squad, and only escaped with her life by showing her passport and insisting that she worked for the American Embassy. She wouldn't admit to blowing up the Mercedes, but the smirk on her face when I brought it up gave her away. About nine in the morning, Charlie pulled up to a wine shop in Healdsburg. We used the torn fifty to buy a thirty-dollar bottle of bubbly and two champagne glasses, and then spent the change on burgers at the drive-in in Cloverdale. We celebrated her return and my narrow escape until about Ukiah, when I plunged into a deep sleep.

\* \* \* \* \* \* \*

I could have slept forever, but for the faint hint of sage growing outside that nudged me on my way to consciousness. It took a blissfully long time for my senses to awaken, led by my nose, which searched the air for the pleasantly familiar smell. Charlie was curled up on my chest, beginning to wake at the same time. We were kissing before we opened our eyes. They were long kisses to make up for the months of kisses lost. One kiss melted into another, until there was no beginning and no end—hunger giving way to passion only after the fear of going on alone had eased. Finally, when the elusive love thing happened, it transcended sex and became some other indefinable thing that finds expression only in your lover's eyes. Charlie rolled onto me and slowly rocked away the fear. She was truly a lifesaver.

I stayed in the bed when Charlie left the trailer we had slept in. As she left, she put Europe '72 on the stereo, and I listened to "Morning Dew" until I was ready to get up. Throwing on some shorts and a loose shirt, I ventured outside onto a desert-like property somewhere in Northern California. Dry shrubs and yucca lined the box canyon we were parked in. I made my way to the shaded porch of a large cabin next to the trailer. As I climbed the steps, I heard women laughing, and as I approached the screen door, I was almost floored by the smell of marijuana. Inside were four of Charlie's "housewife" crew, including Tina Wilson, who had become well settled in the area. Sitting cross-legged around a large pile of my indoor crop, they were talking and laughing as they trimmed. I noticed a glass table with a large pile of coke to the right of the door as I entered. All of the women had a drink going, except Charlie, who had just awakened. However, she was amped up pretty well already, and they were cutting through that weed in a hurry. I said good morning to the ladies, most of whom I knew. They quickly hipped me to the time, 4 p.m. I made my way over to Charlie, who was sitting in a wooden rocking chair across the room. In an alcove behind her were my two crops, nicely separated and drying on screens.

One of the girls held up an immature bud and asked, "Hey, Jason, what the hell kind of shit is this?"

"It's the kind of shit the cops didn't get," I replied, laughing smugly. I asked Charlie if we were safe here for a while. She said we could stay as long as we wanted, and no one could find us. She hadn't called the city to find out what was going on, but I shouldn't worry. Riiight!

I found a comfortable spot out on the porch to sit down, which tugged on my bandages just enough to remind me of the night before. It hurt, but I was feeling invincible. What were the possibilities? Where could we plant next? Images of *ganja* forests floated in my mind. Gardens in the trees, gardens underground, or even better, gardens under water. No matter how they attacked us, we'd find a way to plant the seed that would save the world. We'd supply the hungry lungs of millions of like-minded true believers. We'd cure the sick and feed the hungry. We'd—"

"Hey, hey, hey! Wait a minute! Just a damn minute!" It was the Narrator, just in time. "Catch a breath, will you? The sun is warm, the breeze is perfect, the money is in the shoebox, and the woman loves you. Relax!"

For once, I would listen to the voice. Breathing deeply, I removed my shirt and moved into the sunlight, closing my eyes to its brightness. Visions of the raven danced inside my eyelids. The voice was right. It was all too glorious.

# CHAPTER 10

I should have left well enough alone. What was it about this plant that could drive a man so? I felt its power there with me wherever I was. Was it leading or following? I didn't know, but it had revealed this life for the dream that it really is. That in itself should have been enough, but somehow after only two years of being gardenless, I was somewhat at a loss as to what to do with the rest of my life. The hermit's lifestyle I had adopted, while it was certainly the best thing for me, had left my blood running slow. Though I spent my days and nights in near solitude in the peace of those mountains, there was an angst that ran hot and cold in me and sometimes burned like a fever.

It wasn't the money, for surely the cash I had salted away was more than I had ever had before. Nor the fame, for that was the grower's biggest ogre. One might say the thrilling possibility—dare I say likelihood—of getting caught was the driving force, but I assure you, as one who has been haunted by the fear of that persecution for nearly the whole of my life, that was far from the case. But there we might have stumbled onto the key that turns this twisted lock. It might have been that the very persecution of who we were—of who we had become—that inspired us to raise that peaceful herb as the flag over our sovereignty. For make no mistake, it was really us they hated. Us they feared. There really was a cultural war going on in America, but only one side was fighting.

I had taken to those woods for solace in the form of a rigorous exercise regimen, consisting of long, cross-country runs of my own design. It usually took the better part of a day and ended up at either the river or a favorite grove of redwoods that stands cathedral-like near the top of a very steep grade. On occasion, I have climbed nearly a hundred feet up one of the southernmost giants in that grove, from which perch, on a fog free day, I could clearly see the ocean some thirty miles away. In the tradition of Walker, I had recognized each full moon, save the first, with all-night psychedelic jaunts into the wilderness. All of this was good for body and soul, but did little to deter the gnashing of teeth that was gnawing at my psyche.

It wasn't until I had a visit from an old friend—who had long since fallen into disfavor due to certain unsavory qualities and now wanted to mend some long-fallen fences—that my resolve faded. I had decided never again to trust this smooth-talking, highly manipulative old buddy, and in a short time, it became clear that he hadn't changed a bit in these many years. I would have just blown Kent off, but he came to smoke the peace pipe, knowing that this being a kind of offering from his spirit to mine I would never refuse. Then to my surprise, he produced a joint that smelled, tasted, and, lo and behold, smoked exactly like Elvis the King... our long-lost strain that we feared had been busted out of existence.

The Weed That Killed Elvis was a curious strain, to say the least. We had been growing it for years, and no one we knew had ever seen a seed or a male. It was an unknown strain of cuttings we bought from a friend to fill up the warehouse. The plants looked beautiful, but we thought nothing of it until we grew them side by side with several other strains. With thin leaves and dense buds, it was obviously a cross of some kind, but even with its tendency to bolt when stressed and the immense crystal content, its origin was difficult to place. Besides its different look, it had a unique, almost toxic, taste. Unlike other herbs, its powerful flavor could put off the uninitiated, but seemed like an old friend the second time around. As for potency, suffice it to say, it was right up there with the best weeds in the world. With grand, slow expansion and a high that seemed to affect the equilibrium. Many casual smokers wished they hadn't smoked as much.

Growers and smokers have been known to go on and on about the qualities of their favorite strain, so I'll try not to go there. I only want to impress on you the extent to which a large group of Bay Area pot smokers and I had become attached to this specific plant. Elvis had made quite a name for itself amongst local artists, musicians, and herb aficionados before those flak-jacketed, black-booted thugs kicked the doors off our indoor Eden and wiped all known traces of the weed that killed Elvis off the planet.

So you can imagine the shock to my half-heartedly retired nervous system when that familiar smoke drifted my way. I wanted to jump up and shout, "Do you know what you have here?! Do you understand that you alone possess this nearly eradicated holy smoke?!" But it was obvious that the importance of Elvis—the power of the brand—was of my own making, and letting Kent in on the secret would only give him renewed opportunities to manipulate me. Knowing that the only way to deal with the game of a manipulator was to win, I simply mustered my best Elvis accent and said, "Thank you. Thank you very much!"

Well, that was the bale that broke the burro's back. All that valiant effort I put into my forced retirement was washed away in an avalanche of renewed desire. In that moment, history was writing itself with little concern for my mortal circumstance. In an instant, it was clear that my mission, no matter the cost, would be to secure the Elvis and provide for its ongoing survival, thereby saving the strain from police extinction.

There was no decision for me to make, but I was confident that Charlie wouldn't be so sure. She had made a Herculean effort to make me comfortable in my self-imposed exile because she knew the rules as well as I. Don't get greedy! Listen to your gut feeling. And even though my better judgment told me to stay safe in the serenity of those woods, I knew I had to go.

❋    ❋    ❋    ❋    ❋    ❋    ❋

That night, I made plans with Drake to return to the East Bay and begin at once to rebuild and restart his garden. He had been begging for my help for months and was as excited as a bookie on payday to get her going again. When I carefully broached the subject with Charlie during our quiet dinner for two, rather than the expected tongue-lashing or solemn looks of disappointment, she thought it was a great idea! It would do me good to dabble, she said. To get outta the sticks. I didn't know what to think of this change of heart, but seeing the opening, I pushed right through. "I might be gone a couple of weeks," I added.

"You just go do what you gotta do. Make the world safe for marijuana," she said, dismissing the subject and giving me the feeling that my bags were already packed.

As I crossed the coastal ridge towards Highway 101, leaving redwood country, I had that feeling of, "I know I shouldn't be doing this"—the one I promised never to ignore again. As I headed down 101, I resolved to be extra careful to follow all traffic laws and, most importantly, not to smoke till I passed Cloverdale. The cops had been stopping hundreds of cars indiscriminately—or for whatever minor infraction they could invent, like a dirty license plate or long hair. Then they searched the cars of those supposed traffic offenders with drug-sniffing dogs and ran their driver's licenses, and whattaya' know, they managed to get about a forty-percent arrest rate. What could be easier, more profitable, or safer than busting potheads? And sure enough, the roadway was swarming with C.H.P. and the like, but I managed to navigate safely through all the little highway towns and was highly relieved when I reached the freeway. After so long in the forest, the multiple lanes, oncoming traffic, and commotion of the city took a little getting used to, but, as in the forest, one could hide in the confusion. There was anonymity in the crowd. And in time, being of the city, my urban animal instincts awakened, reminding me of the cocaine-edge existence that is city life. At once demoralizing and intoxicating.

When I got to Drake's house, I found him in a froth. He had completed moving the small truckload of gear from its hiding place back into the secret room we had built under his house, which was no easy task. Now he was hurriedly trying to assemble the pieces like some madman answering only to the voices in his head. He wanted to resurrect the sixteen-light project and plant the best seeds available, immediately! I had my own agenda, but since it would take longer to fill the room with Elvis, we compromised on a plan to grow one long cycle from seed first. That would give me four full months to acquire and establish new Elvis moms.

That turned out to be easier to say. My old friend Kent felt a momentum shift in our relationship the instant he received my phone call. He began to try to take advantage of his newfound pry-bar during our very first meeting at his house later that day when I tried to lock down his entire harvest. All one-point-two pounds of it. Sensing my eagerness, he played it for all it was worth, insisting I pay top dollar for the entire thing at the ounce price. When I was not deterred by that, he complained that he didn't like to do all the trimming at once, so if I really wanted the whole thing at one time, I'd have to dry and trim it myself. I knew the idea of me sitting around trimming his pot all day was the kind of power trip he couldn't resist, so I decided to play into it. Knowing full well that I had trimmed my last bud ever, I decided to get someone else to trim it and pay him or her out of Kent's end. So I agreed, and I praised him relentlessly on the power of his weed. I'm sure he suspected that the day he turned over cuttings would be the last day he ever saw me. Still, having that kind of power over me was irresistible, and in the end he knew he would have to cough up some plants. It took a full two months of spitting out his stems and leaf, stroking his ego, and taking his shit before I convinced him that it was not only disrespectful to me, but downright immoral to horde the King. He finally kicked down two bedraggled but still living baby girls, which I rushed into intensive care at Drake's house, managing to save only one, which grew healthy enough to take cuttings from. Those first six cuttings became the new mother plants that would provide the hundreds of clones it would take to replenish our garden. I haven't seen Kent since.

During that time, I moved into Drake's house, sleeping on a mattress in the garden's work area. You would think that the whirring of fans and buzzing ballasts clicking on and off would bother me, but those distractions were like lullabies to me now. I was comforted by the sticky smell and humid air and could sleep quite soundly amongst the plants. In fact, the buzz was spurring me on like an extra cup of coffee, keeping me ready to pounce in that feline-like state of mind necessary to the art of urban growing.

We babied our six precious Elvis moms for months, taking only those cuttings that were ready and doting over their every need for another six weeks. Meanwhile in the bloom room, seeds of several varieties like the Haze, SK-1, and Northern Lights-5 matured to fruition. It was a very spicy harvest requiring much comparative smoking, but it took longer than anticipated, causing us to top and prune the waiting Elvis cuttings into large bushes with only an inch between nodes and long bottom branches that reached for the light. We had to cram them in at four to a light, creating an impenetrable wall of green. No light reached the floor. After replanting the bloom room, we transplanted rooted starts into the moms' room to beef up and immediately refilled the clone box with fresh-cut clones. Drake was immensely pleased. With fresh harvest and a sea of green to follow, all was well in his world. And I had accomplished my mission to save the Elvis, my fatherless friend, from extinction or a fate worse than death—a life of not being fully appreciated. Drake assured me a small share of the garden would be mine, so I requested the top three inches. But the idea of hanging around to run the show seemed like going over old ground. Little challenge with lots of risk. No, that would be bending the rules too far. I called Charlie to tell her I'd be coming home after the Jerry Garcia show at the Warfield Theater the following night, but she didn't seem too excited at the news, causing me to wonder again what was up with her. The rest of the conversation was hurried and rather matter-of-fact, and in just moments, I was left with a dead receiver in my hand.

It seemed like a good time to let loose, and there was no place better for that than the Jerry Show. Everything seemed to be in its place, and an escape window had opened. I'd make it back to the woods after a short side-trip into Dead-land. I was a little paranoid by nature, but I had been to enough of those shows to be very comfortable in there. Bongs and rolling trays on every other table raised the comfort level even further. I usually liked to start the evening by lighting five or six joints consecutively, thereby pacifying the entire section, all people I would soon be bumping into. Having thusly eased all tension in the air, the moment would be prepared for a little wild dancin' and whoopin' and hollerin'. A kindly looking gentleman in casual tie-dye garb with a colorful knit cap was standing to my left, and since I normally pass to that direction, he was the lucky beneficiary of good fate, accepting his lot with bleary-eyed enthusiasm. I later learned his name was Bernie, though he said it was Mountain, and by the time Jerry finished "The Way You Do the Things You Do," Mountain and I had already do-sidoed our way to breathless laughter. By halfway through the first set, the crowd was mixing it up real good, and I had lost sight of my new friend, but that made little difference to me, as by then the drugs were beginning to kick in. I was fending off the uncomfortable paranoia that attends losing your mind by furiously dancing through it and doing the conscious breathing that is necessary if one is to sustain that level of exertion for three-plus hours. But I was willing to be a little discomfited. It was worth it. Because this wasn't just a lark. I was after something here. There was something truly cataclysmic that happened on rarified occasions when you mixed endorphins and LSD. When you took it through what long-distance runners call "the wall" and found that you were no longer out of breath or tired. A happiness overload. A kind of joy breakdown, where you are happier than anyone has a right to be. Sweating, crying, and laughing in unison and to the beat. Grateful to be alive. But before one is reborn, there must necessarily be a death. In this case, the death of the self, and after "Deal" reached its dizzying crescendo, they turned on the house lights, revealing a theater full of these grateful dead—crazed, and winded and all riding the same hallucination.

It was some time before I felt capable of having a conversation, but I did the best I could to converse with the others at my table during the intermission. I managed only a few nods and uh-huhs before I turned to my little, green, joint bottle to take the edge off the situation. Yes, I'd leave it to the herb to say all the words my better self would say if my tongue weren't so twisted. I lit one and, without thinking, passed it too soon. One J in a group that size would probably never return, so I decided not to wait and lit another right away. Mountain perked right up and assumed his position, but this time I held onto it for a good while. This was one of those times when herb was most useful. Like a river of calm, it filled me up. The rising smoke obscured the crazy eyes behind. On the outside, I struggled to regain composure while obtuse faces streamed words at me, but inside, I was counting the nanoseconds until the music started again. As Peter Lorre once said, "I can't stand being around so many people—when they're alive." The moment the show began again, I slipped back into the aisles to be alone in the crowd. Now, deadheads were a real loose bunch anyway, but with me dancing like a wild emu high on electricity right next to them, even the stiffest of the hand-in-pocket set began to get their groove on. By the time Jerry let into "Don't Let Go," he had the whole place whipped to a froth, especially in our section, where a few of us were going stark-raving bonkers dancing and laughing our way into oxygen debt. I stopped ten minutes into the spacey part to catch my breath and wipe the sweat from my face. It was not the cataclysmic joy meltdown I was aiming for, but I was having a great show, that is, until Mountain appeared out of the shadows right beside me. I was still grinning like a crazed fool and in the middle of changing into a dry shirt when I noticed the forced smile on his face, kind of through his teeth, and I sensed nervousness about him. His demeanor had changed. He stood upright in a defensive stance and looked right into my eyes like a crazed tweeker on a three-day binge. "I'm supposed to deliver a message to you," he said, "from a mutual friend." I didn't know what he was talking about, but I could see by that look that he was deadly serious. "He's got an important job for you," he continued.

"Fortunately, I don't need a job," I said sarcastically. I tried to breeze by him and return to dancing up and down the aisles, where the ushers had long since disappeared or joined in, but he blocked my path.

"Hey, what's yer fuckin' problem?!" I squawked.

"My problem?" He had to look up to lock me in his stare. "I can't believe he would ever work with a flaky, fuckin' security risk like you."

Still not correctly assessing the situation, I cracked wise, "Oh, I don't know, I feel pretty secure." That was obviously the wrong thing to say. I saw the flash of the knife as he withdrew it from the buckle of his belt, but before I could react, a forearm and elbow slammed into my chest with plenty of weight behind them, sliding firmly into my neck, crashing me into the kitchen wall behind, and pinning me into a darkened corner. At once I felt the knife pinch the skin under my ribcage.

"You wanna be funny?" he said, with pure malice in his voice. "You think this is funny?" He forced me further into the wall, putting pressure on my windpipe, cutting off my air. "I can't believe you would even work with this idiot," he muttered psychotically into thin air, then turned back to me to finish the sentence, "but he says you are the man, so get this straight." He was really angry now and right up in my face. "A lot of people are counting on you, you little asshole, so you better straighten up and do as you're told." He jammed a piece of paper into my hip pocket and growled, "Be there."

By now, I was getting pretty pissed off, and, realizing that he wasn't going to kill me, I got indignant, "This is no fuckin' way to deliver a fuckin' message," I snipped. "I'll go wherever the fuck I want, whenever the fuck I want to." He slowly pushed the knife against my stomach and used his arm to force me all the way to the floor. Withdrawing the knife, he swiftly slipped it under my belt and cut my waist pack right off me. I grabbed at it, but he put his boot on my bare chest and held the pack out of my reach. He smiled that nervous grin again as he pushed his foot into me. "You'll be there," he hissed. Then the smile disappeared, and he warned me, "Don't get up." He stomped me one time for good measure, causing my eyes to close momentarily. When they opened only a second later, he had vanished.

It took a moment to compose myself. The acid I had been riding had turned to adrenaline coursing through my body. No one around me had noticed a thing. That guy could have finished me right there, and no one would have been the wiser! But why? I reached into my pocket to find the note. I struggled in the dark to read it, but I had already correctly assumed who it was from. "Meet me in spot number four, three o'clock tomorrow, signed, your pal." I sat there stewing in my own pot of fuming anger for a few minutes, watching the hundreds of blissed-out revelers absorb the sweet gospel of "Like A Road." Chester Hawthorne had gone too far this time! There could be no excuse for this kind of behavior. Even if I was a blow-it case, hey, I was supposed to be a retired blow-it case. I reached for my green bottle. "Damn it!" Not only did he have my wallet, but my whole stash as well. Then, realizing that I was the only angry person in the building, I got up and hustled myself out of the theater in a huff, well before Jerry shredded the end of "Tangled Up in Blue." Having learned my lesson, though, I chose the back door to make my exit.

# CHAPTER 11

Spot number four was a public bathroom in one of the parks in the hills above Oakland and Berkeley. It was one of Chet's favorite meeting places, not just because it was very remote, but mainly because it locked from the inside. It was only for one person, but it was wheelchair accessible, so it was very large. Except for the concrete floor, the entire room, walls, and fixtures were made of stainless steel and kept very clean. It had the feel of a vault. There were no cars in the lot when I got to the park—not a soul moving anywhere—but I knew as I approached the john that he was out there in the woods somewhere, watching. The door was locked, but Chet had had a key made, which I retrieved from its nearby hiding place, and in moments I was inside. I flicked on the florescent lights just as the door closed, expecting to wait for Chet. Instead, I found a box the size of a nineteen-inch TV wrapped package-like in brown paper and tied with a plain, white string. There were no markings to identify it, save an old Memorex cassette tape marked "Deep Purple" and a manila envelope sitting right on top.

Beside the box lay a bundle of neatly folded laundry wrapped in tissue and my cleanly severed waist pack, stash intact. I was all ready to chew him out, but he wasn't going to let me. He wouldn't even show. Instead, I got a surprise package, which I was sure couldn't be good. But as angry as I was, the Mission Impossible instruction cassette brought a smile to my face. I could hear the words, "Good morning, Mr. Phelps," as if Chet were right inside my head. There was nothing to play it on except the car stereo, so I had to take the box with me. I could feel myself being dragged around by the nose. Exiting the outhouse with that mystery box made me feel very conspicuous, but I made it to the car and down the road before inserting the tape.

"Hi, pal!" were the first words. They were words I knew to be Chet's, but in the voice of a very old lady. "Sorry about the run-around, but it was unavoidable." I couldn't help but wonder where he got this old lady from. "I need a favor, old chum. Can you help me out?" Very convenient for him that I couldn't answer. "I know you are retired and all that, but I simply require your advice on a matter of great import! Please meet me in the Mission, at La Taqueria, near the northeast corner of Twenty-Sixth Street. Four p.m. And pal"—there was more—"one more thing. Please deliver this box to this man…" Inside the envelope I found an eight-by-ten glossy of the guy. "Half an hour before you meet me, he will be walking out the front door of the building at 2601 Mission Street, on the southwest corner. At exactly three-thirty. He will walk directly to his car parked in the lot that serves the building. A brown Lincoln Town Car." Pictures of the building and the car were included. "He will expect you, but he won't wait around, so don't be late. Just say your pal sent you, put the box in his trunk, and say good-bye. And pal," he paused a little too long, "you gotta wear these clothes." I unwrapped the clothing and found the dress uniform of a marine lieutenant. Then, as if his word was enough to pre-empt my legitimate concerns, he added, "Believe me, my friend, there is nothing illegal in the box, and no harm will come to you." He didn't even have to tell me not to look. He knew I wouldn't. This all seemed strange coming from my grandmother's voice, but we both knew I'd be there.

Back at Drake's, I lay awake most of the night wondering what the hell Chet was up to, knowing that whatever it was, he hadn't thought I would readily agree to it. The caution lights were blinking in my head when I finally went to sleep.

\* \* \* \* \* \* \*

There was no need to get up early the next day, as both my meetings would be in the afternoon. But I awoke at the crack of dawn anyway, because I was nervous as a hen at a cockfight about the mission. I trusted Chet completely, but that box was giving me the shakes. Why me? He must have had a hundred folks who could have made that drop. Maybe he was just testing me, and the box was full of newspaper. At any rate, I steeled myself to the task and tried to put it out of my mind by working in Drake's garden. He gave me the honor of harvesting and cloning, while he did all the planting, saving me from having to deal with itchy rock wool fibers getting into my skin or eyes. Harvesting gave me a chance to examine every bud and be very familiar with what was going on in the room. Plus, it was very therapeutic, allowing me to get lost in the moment rather than worrying about the future. The future comes soon enough.

I got to the meeting site early, as is my wont, to take a look around. A perfectly normal day with lots of people in the street. While I waited in a parking spot on the boulevard adjacent to the lot, I watched the comings and goings outside the building and checked the parked cars for possible surveillance. I was suspicious of everything, from loiterers to PG&E trucks, but there was nothing suspect there. No excuse that would allow me to blow the whole thing off. So I changed into the uniform and waited in my van for the gentleman to appear at the front steps. When he did, right on time, I exited my side door with the box, crossed the walk, and appeared beside his trunk at the instant he arrived. He was a stocky guy, on the short side, with a kind of Poncho Villa mustache and longish sideburns that didn't quite match his very well-coiffed, straight, black hair. A thousand-dollar suit and grotesque, diamond pinky ring glorified the look, but he still looked like a Mexican spook. Not a gregarious man at all, he just opened up the trunk for the box and didn't reply at all when I mentioned that his "pal" had sent me. I left some boot tread getting back to my van, and then got the hell out of there. I didn't like this guy's manner, and I could sense danger, even if Chet denied it. And I couldn't wait to get out of that monkey suit. A half-hour later, Chet arrived at La Taqueria where we were to meet in a souped-up 1965 Nova Super Sport. He had it painted the most obscure shade of beige/tan he could get them to mix. He called it camel-colored and claimed it made the car damn near invisible. However ugly it was on the outside, the interior was fantastic. Trick Volvo seats were bolted to the frame, with the kind of extra-wide seatbelt straps they use on Jeeps. The dash and console were hand-carved cherry wood and hid two built-in stash places. Toggle switches on the dash controlled front and taillights separately, allowing him to disappear from the view of pursuing vehicles. With a big, bored-out, 427-cubic-inch engine and high performance everything in such a tiny car, it was faster than shit, and having completed the Bondurant School of Driving at Sears Point Raceway, he was ready to race. He revved it up a little, showing off, as I got in. After throwing his brim and a thirty-five-millimeter camera in the back seat, he went through a ritual of seat adjustment and switch flipping that would tire a helicopter pilot before pulling into traffic with a screech and busting gears all the way to the freeway.

We headed east out of town at just about dark, through the suburbs, and into the San Joaquin Valley. This gave me plenty of time to rag on him about my ill treatment. He swore it was acid induced paranoia that made Mountain freak out and by the time we got to Tracy, he had satisfied me with apologies and explanations and more fantastic promises. Before we reached the foothills of the Sierra, he blindfolded me with a pair of blacked-out, side-blinder sunglasses, and after another hour of downshifting into turns and powering out of them, the Nova rolled to a stop. I removed the glasses and stepped out of the car into some kind of warehouse garage with a big loading dock that had room for three eighteen-wheelers. The only light came from a ring of windows along three walls just under the thirty-foot ceiling. The floor was covered with sawdust, which I assumed was to pick up oil dropped by the trucks, but judging by the lack of tracks, no trucks had been there for a while. Outside there was the noise of a lot of machinery cranking and trucks moving around, but I had no idea where we were. Chet led me to a freight elevator in one corner, and the sound of the gate closing echoed throughout the garage, highlighting just how big and empty it was. "This is our space," Chet said, with that we're-gonna-make-a-fortune grin on his face. He had to use a key to work the elevator. Then he pushed the button for level two, and the wooden-floored lift began to lower, passing through a good ten feet of concrete before reaching the first underground floor. The gate opened into a small storage room only about ten-by-twenty feet containing a desk and a chair and plenty of shelves, but looking rather unused. Chet wasted no time crossing to a set of double doors on the far side of the room, where he paused just long enough to flash me a very mischievous look, then threw the doors open and disappeared into thousands of watts of metal-halide light. It surged in, consuming all the oxygen around my eyes, causing them to shrivel against the onslaught. "Come into the light," a mocking voice said. "Don't be afraid." As I did, my eyes adjusted, and the room came into focus. It was immense, with a twelve-foot-high ceiling. Forty feet wide on the short side and longer than I could make out, seeing as there were dozens of lamps in the way, over a forest of plants in various stages of disrepair. The sheer size of it was a chin-dropper, and it was all I could do to act nonchalant. No less than sixty lights in five rows of twelve sat on five-foot centers. Twenty-five hundred square feet under production, plus a room for moms and clones at the far end. I perused the aisles, checking out the plants, while I caught my breath. The Narrator quickly computed the critical figures—number of lights, pounds per light, dollars per pound—and assessed annual yield at one-and-a-half million dollars. Yeouch! "Whataya think?" he asked, anxiously.

"What is this place?" I answered with a question. My answer wasn't as enthusiastic as he had hoped.

He tried again. "We built it to your specifications. Light, temperature, ventilation, everything! And look at this moms' room." We entered the room at the far end of the space. It was complete with a large work area, similar to a kitchen, and a small sleeping area with a real twin bed! The giant clone box took up a whole wall and the whole place was outfitted with top-flight equipment. A pot grower's dream. "Howdaya like that?"

"Sweet," was my heartfelt response.

"The guy who is in this with me is an excellent mechanic. Does electrical, plumbing, carpentry, you-name-it. But he doesn't know shit about growing plants. You see what I mean?" He held up a tray of wilted cuttings.

"They look sad," I said, examining the root cubes. They had yet to root and were beginning to rot. "And when you start with sad babies..." —I pointed to the bloom room and his seriously withered ladies— "... you get really unhappy adults."

"That's why I need your help," he begged. "I need someone who loves pot plants, like you!" He knew how to get to me.

"They *are* suffering," I said continuing to point them out as we walked around the room. Some were rotting on the vine, some damaged by toxic salts or burned by the lights, and all dripping with mites. The room was three-quarters filled, but only one corner, about ten lights, were hardy plants, and they were patchy. "I could grow a fortune in here," I said, ogling his exhaust fan. It was the size of a large ceiling fan, but more durable and mounted vertically into the wall near the moms' room. Its large metal blades weren't spinning fast, but a torrent of air was surging through the opening. The faint smell of charcoal emanating from the fan explained why there were no ozone generators visible. They would have had to be the large size and plenty of them. "Some kind of charcoal filter?" I asked, trying to confirm my theory.

He chuckled slightly, and his face even began to blush when he answered. "Yeah, you could say it is something of a charcoal filter." I sensed there was more to the story, but there would be plenty of time to figure out how the exhaust worked, so long as it did. "Exactly how big a fortune?" he queried, not distracted by my ventilation side-trip.

"It's easily a million-dollar room," I said, not wanting to raise expectations. "Maybe more, if you get somebody good to run it."

"I've got someone good!" he insisted, looking right at me.

"It's tempting, brother. But I'm happily retired," I said, trying to raise my stock. "You know I have infinite love and respect for you, but this is too much work and too much risk for me."

"Oh, yes, you'll do it," he stated flatly. "You'll live and work here full-time. You'll lend us all of your knowledge and expertise, and you'll like it!"

I didn't like the tone of his voice. Not menacing, but over-confident, like a parent to a child. He was my mentor and my friend, but he had seen much evil in his life, and I knew he was capable of justifying harsh tactics in order to get what he wanted, like some kind of benevolent mafia don. "You're awfully sure of yourself," I snipped, carefully asserting my independence.

"I'm absolutely positive of myself." He grinned like a prizefighter who knows he's gonna knock you out. He paused, waiting for my retort. Being not so cocksure of myself as he, I hesitated and, in that instant, lost the stare-down. "Come with me, my fine, weed-growing friend, and let me enlighten you." He put his arm around me and led me to a single door at the end of a small hallway running along the mother room to the back wall of the giant garden. It opened into a wide stairwell that went up a few flights and descended into darkness. He skipped down one flight, hardly able to contain himself. I followed right behind, drawn by the tractor beam of his enthusiasm. Opening a door exactly like the one above, we entered a room directly below the moms' room, which shared its dimensions, but this one was converted into a beautiful studio apartment—the kitchen being in the moms' room upstairs. A fully equipped master bed and bath and living quarters, complete with big-screen entertainment center. It was beautiful. Built with loving care. But it was so exactly like the room above that I couldn't help but wonder what lay on the other side of the interior door. I barely glanced at the apartment before Chet caught me staring at it. "Go ahead," he said. "Check it out." Without a moment of hesitation, I bolted through the door. This time my eyes had to adjust to darkness. Pitch darkness, except for the faint light from the apartment behind me. Chet brushed by me, and after fumbling around a little, he turned on a work light, of the extension-cord variety that was hanging from a wooden ladder in the center of the room. The light was not strong enough to reach into the corners, but it was obviously the same exact room as the one above. Room for another sixty lights! The space was cavernous and raw. Only the huge exhaust fan had been installed, but all of the equipment was already there, brand new, and in boxes piled half-way to the ceiling.

"You're kidding!" I said, not believing my eyes.

"Not only am I not kidding," he said, leaving another pregnant pause that caused me to hold my breath, "there's one more." I shot through the living space, slammed into the stairwell with a crash, then bounded farther down the stairs to the bottom floor and grabbed the door handle. This was no time to remain cool, and no dope grower worth a shit could have. I flung the door open and leapt in. The door

*Top: Sunrise Harvest at Salt Creek;*
*Above & following pages: The colorado*

*Above: Love & Luck;*

*Above: Big Sur Ridge;*
*Left: Haze;*

*Opposite: Elvis; Above: "I won't say" beach; Following page: Swazi*

closed behind me, and I stood still, in black-hole darkness, so as not to disturb the calm. I detected the smell of oil, like at a mechanic's garage, but I heard no sound, not even the scurry of a cockroach, until Chet caught up and opened the door to my rear. The crack of light revealed more boxes of equipment, but these were more like crates, and they were very old. Large pieces of machinery sat here and there, including a large, circular saw-blade six feet in diameter and the now-familiar sawdust on the floor. I turned back to Chet, and he laughed out loud at the look of wonder on my face. "The s-s-same s-s-size r-r-room?" I stuttered. He nodded. "And you can power all this?" He nodded again. I grabbed my head to relieve the ache of understanding. "What the hell is this place?" I shouted a little too loudly. The echo took a while to subside, but the volume didn't unnerve him.

He took out one of his Gauloises cigarettes and lit it in the darkness like some Humphrey Bogart character, exhaled deftly, then spilled the beans. "It's a working lumber mill."

The words ping-ponged around in my head while we returned to the moms' room on the first floor. He was cackling all the way up the stairs, so pleased was he with my dumbfounded reaction. I barely heard a cackle of it though, as the Narrator in my brain was still following the bouncing ball. "A lumber mill! A hundred-and-eighty lights! Five million dollars a year! Whoa, now that was impressive!" It had to be the biggest illicit indoor grow in the world. And I'd be controlling production. Beyond the money, this would be a world-class challenge. It would be an impressive accomplishment and a heroic win for our side. But an operation this size was doomed to fail. Too many people would have to know about it. The workers, the trimmers, the sellers. And, let's face it, karmically, it might just be too greedy. But by the time we settled into the mothers' room, he on the work stool and me on the single sleeper with my back against the bloom-room wall, I had put aside the greater concerns of failure and karma and began firing questions on the mechanics.

"Where will you get the juice to run it all?" was the first and most obvious.

"The mill," he said. "It generates its own power, and we just tap in. Practically unlimited."

I could feel vibrations against my back from the ballasts hung on the opposite side of the wall. "And where does it exhaust?" I asked. "That's a whole lot of stink coming off seventy-five-hundred square feet of ripe buds."

"Those three giant fans are venting into a large shaft that connects directly to one of the mill's huge chimneys. Wood smoke is rising in that chimney twenty-four hours a day, creating a good deal of additional suction. Small bits of ash and burnt wood drift back down the shaft, giving off the charcoal smell, which neutralizes the pot smell. The smoke exits the stack eighty feet above the mill. You see, I've got it all figured out, except one critical element. I need your expertise. I know if you put yourself into this task, you can pull it off. You may be the only one I know who can. We just seem to be spinning our wheels. There's more to it than just building the room and planting the seeds. We need the love, and that's you. It's always been you."

"Yeah, but this thing is doomed for a big fall," I said, my better judgment trying to come to the fore.

"Here's the thing. The kicker." He looked right through my eyes into my head. "It's risk-free."

"How do you figure that?" I snorted. "This baby is built to crash! There's almost no chance of succeeding."

"I guarantee it," he said with pure confidence. "One hundred percent guaranteed safe."

"No way! Not possible!" I replied.

"Oh, yes," he said. "Absolutely possible. In fact, it's a lock. I'll guarantee your safety. And I'll guarantee your salary. How's half-a-million?"

Those were pretty outlandish claims had they been coming from anyone but Chester Hawthorne. He was one man whose words I rarely questioned, for he had made many wild promises to me in the past and had always fulfilled or exceeded each one. But this was the wildest and most impossible feat ever. If it were true—a dream project and guaranteed salary, risk-free—I knew I could not refuse, and he knew it too. Now that we both knew I was a whore, the only question was... how much? "What would my responsibility be?" I asked.

"It would be your baby," he exclaimed, knowing the hook had been set. "You run the show with my guy working at your direction. This would be your fiefdom. I'd be responsible for bringing in everything you need and bringing out the product. Believe me," he continued, "we've tried it without you, and if we could get away with it, we would. I have no desire to cut you in, but at this point, we've discovered it's crucial."

Now Chet was a world-class negotiator, and "critical" and "crucial" are not words he normally used in a salary bargain, so it was evident that I had him over a barrel. "Okay, assuming I take this gig," I said, "there would be a few requirements." I decided to go for the throat to see just how far his desperation would get me. "First of all, this is a five-million-dollar garden, and if I'm going to give one-hundred-percent of my time and energy to this project, I'm going to need more than a ten-percent salary. That's an insult."

"I don't want to be insulting," he said. "What sounds right to you?"

"Well, normally I'd work for an even share." I had to try.

"Impossible," he replied calmly. "I got the building and solved all the major problems. I procured the equipment. I'm distributing the product and guaranteeing your security. I have expenses you can't imagine..." he started to get hurt.

"Okay, okay," I interrupted. "Then I'll want a guaranteed million!" After pausing to think, he conceded. "I can stretch it that far, but you'd better produce!"

"Oh, I'll produce all right, but if I produce significantly more than five million, I'm gonna need a performance bonus."

"Like what? A percentage of the over?" He was getting irritated.

"I'll leave the size of my bonus up to you." I didn't want to push. "Suffice it to say, if I make you very happy, you make me very happy."

"Done!" he exclaimed, jumping up to shake on it.

"Wait just a minute," I said. "I'm not done yet. I'll need help. There is no way I can do this alone, even if I stay here night and day."

"I have my guy as your helper. You can teach him as you go," he responded quickly.

"No! I'll burn out," I said. "I'll need someone who knows what he is doing to help carry the load, someone who can relieve me when I'm burnt. You just can't understand how taxing this can be. Especially at this level. No, I'll defInitely need to have my own guy in there at a cost of another five-hundred-thousand bucks. It's a deal breaker."

"I'll pay him two-fifty. Anything more will have to come from your end." He started to fume. "Now, whadaya say?"

"Well, I have a few more points of concern," I continued, much to his chagrin.

"Yeah, what else?"

"Where will you sell it?" I mean, twelve-hundred pounds of the good each year—There ought to be plenty of that to go around," I tried to get in through the back door.

"That's my problem. Why don't you come to the point?" he quipped.

"The point is... I want the top of the crop." Now I was getting greedy.

"No way!" he demanded. "I have a safe way to sell it that won't lead back here. You can take all the prime stash you want, but no one else sells this crop! That cuts into my security precautions."

"But..." I would have tried again to persuade him, but he cut me off.

"No way!" he repeated in a manner I recognized to be final.

"What about trimming and drying?" I decided to try another angle.

"That's my department, too," he said.

"Well, as you know," I reminded him gently. "I have this crew of ladies who have a world of experience and a great place. You're going to need a big place that's safe." I tried my damnedest to get Charlie in on it.

He rejected me. "T&D is my thing. Never you mind!"

"It's just that..." I tried again.

"No!" he insisted loudly.

"Hey, just hear me out, would ya?" His face softened, so I continued. "It's just that I wanted them to collect all of the trichomes that fall off in the trimming process, and these girls have it down to a science."

"Trichomes?" he asked.

"Yes, the crystalline dust that sugar-coats the herb. It falls off during the trimming process, and if collected properly, it's the strongest stash of all." My passion for finger hash made itself evident.

"Oh, I don't care about that," he said disgustedly. "You can have your 'trichromiums,' but I'm setting up the T&D. It's part of security, and that's final."

So I couldn't get Charlie in. It would have gone a long way towards convincing her to go along, but it was useless to try further. I had gotten the hash, however, which I knew would be considerable, and a million-dollar salary. That was over eighty-thousand monthly, not to mention over twenty grand a month for JJ. I was feeling pretty good about myself. Confident that I had all the angles covered. So I answered smugly when he asked if I was ready to meet my new partner. "Sure thing, professor." Hell, with the deal I had struck, once I got this apprentice guy trained, I could bug out after a year with a cool million off the top regardless of the actual yield.

"He's real handy to have around," he said, punching the guy's pager number into the phone, "and he's a smart fella, too, so I imagine he'll be a quick study. Like I said, he can do electrical and plumbing and is very good with all things of the mechanical persuasion. He may not have the greenest thumb in the world, but he is absolutely critical to the success of our thing..." There was a knock at the door, and Chet sidestepped over to get it, never taking his eyes off mine as he finished his sentence, "...you see, his father owns this mill," he said as the door opened and in walked my new partner.

"Jason, you remember Patrick."

\*        \*        \*        \*        \*        \*        \*

We shook hands, and he said something about being glad to see me again and wasn't this going to be great. I'm sure I said something pleasant, but I was on automatic, trying to conceal my surprise while I could feel Chet's penetrating gaze scanning for my reaction. I couldn't stop thinking about it the whole six-hour ride back to Charlie's mountain retreat. The entire scene was stuck in my brain like the sunspot that imprinted itself on my eyeballs when Chet cranked open the garage's outside door. We went for a short walking tour around the garage, which was attached to the mill but kind of off to the side. All activity relating to the mill was centered on the other side of the complex. It was only thirty yards of gravel to the tree line, which the trucks used to circle the mill on their way out, making the area just outside the doors quite dusty and noisy. Plenty of people and vehicles moving around, but nobody paying any attention to us or our building. Damned if everything wasn't just as Chet said. The mill, the stacks, the generators, everything. This made me feel reassured about my decision to join up. If he said risk-free, then by God it was risk-free. As I reached the dirt road that led the last four miles to Charlie's place, I became more anxious. She was an adventurous woman, no doubt, but she didn't like people going back on their promises, and I had promised to quit. She was doing her part by keeping her outlaw activities to a minimum, and I didn't think she would want to play housefrau while

I ran around playing with fire. This job, luck willing, would go on for years, demanding most of my attention. I could not think of a good way to break it to her, so I stalled. We had that good long-time-gone sex and took a long walk in the woods where we held hands and giggled like puppy lovers. No time seemed to be the right time, although she kept looking at me as if she expected me to say something. All through dinner and the long snuggle before bed, I kept my secret, until the next morning when she looked at me so expectantly that I just had to take my shot. "Honey," I said in that I-got-bad-news-for-you voice, "there is something that I have to talk to you about." She practically held her breath. "The other day when I was in the city, I ran into Chet." I checked her eyes, but no reaction. "It seems he has a job for me." I thought I'd start off small.

"He does? What's that?" she asked.

"Well, you know, my old work. It's a really good deal for us," I said, trying to include her.

"For us?" she asked.

"Well, for me," I said, "but me is us."

"You're going back to the garden?" The disappointment I expected wasn't evident.

"I can't really say what, but it is going to take quite a bit of my time."

"And you agreed to this job?" She had a tone of excitement I wasn't prepared for.

"Well, no. No, I didn't. I said I thought I should talk it over with you."

"Oh, of course you can," she insisted. "I told you it was all right with me."

"You said it was okay to dabble. This is more like full time."

"Go, play, have fun," she said. I started to get that feeling again, of being pushed out the door.

"No, you don't understand, honey," I tried again. "This is not for fun. It's the real deal. High risk, high gain."

"Sweetheart, you do whatever you think is right." She kept it up. No questions, no cautions to be careful, no nothing. This was not like her.

"I have thought about it a lot, and I am having trouble deciding," I said, wondering how far her newfound change of heart would go. "In fact, I'm thinking about turning him down. It's just too risky and might compromise our relationship beyond repair."

At this, she became worried. "Oh, sweetie, you have to go. If you stayed cooped up here on my behalf, I would never forgive myself. No, you go do what you need to do."

This was amazing. Never had so sure-minded a woman as Charlie made such a complete turnaround in so short a time. "Are you sure, honey?"

Now she turned on the sex, slithering up my body as we lay on the couch. This was normally the way she got her way, not the way I got mine. "I want you to," she said in a hot, sultry voice while rubbing her body the length of mine. She smiled sensuously as she came in for the kill... I mean the kiss.

I couldn't believe this. I was going to get my way *and* get laid. I guess that's what they call having your cake and eating it, too. The Narrator was warning me that something was wrong here. Very wrong. But I was lost in the arms of this temptress. Someplace I would forever be lost. She made love to me that morning as though it was the last time. It was wild, passionate, almost violent, as she practically threw me around the bed from position to position, rifling off instructions on what to touch next as if it would never be touched again. It was strange and exciting, so much so that I lost all track of reason until the next day, when the question hit me as I was looking at her smiling and waving in the rearview mirror. Just why would she reward me by fucking my brains out when I had broken our promise and nearly our relationship?

# CHAPTER 12

It was Winston who put me back in touch with my lifetime co-conspirator after more than a year. First with a wrong telephone number—which turned out to be a beeper owned by an unfriendly gentleman by the name of Judd—then with the address to a beach cottage on the Twenty-Sixth Street beach in Santa Cruz and instructions to enter from the beach side. It was a glorious morning for driving over the mountains from the Bay Area. Beaming sunshine and fresh ocean air. In fact, it was nice all the way through town right up to about half a mile from the beach, where the fog took over and cast a dreary hue. I had to climb a small cliff to get to the back door of his place. It was a cottage all right. A two-bedroom cottage that, though it was small, sat on a half-acre of sculpted lawns and perfectly kept gardens. The picturesque, wood-shingle house, one story with a loft, was set back a hundred feet or so from the cliff. It had large, framed windows in the main room facing the water, making me feel like an armed intruder as I tiptoed across the backyard grass. Perhaps I was on the wrong property altogether, I thought, until I reached the back door. I found it ajar, with the subtle strains of Johnny Winter oozing out at a volume just a little too loud for nine a.m. on a Monday. That had to be him. I gave the door a push, but it was jammed up against something I feared was his dead body. It turned out to be simply a crumpled throw rug, but with Jungle Jim, you never knew. Inside looked like the morning after Animal House. Paper blinds pulled over the ocean view windows gave the room a golden glow, as daylight tried to shine through, the effect heightened by the hours-old cigarette smoke lingering in dead air, inspiring a kind of purgatory-ish feel. But if this was heaven, it was a heaven for drunks, as beer cans ruled the roost. And not good beer, either, but whatever buck-and-a-half-a-six-pack brand was on sale. Pabst Blue Ribbon, Hamm's, or Busch, it didn't make a difference. Beer cans lined every surface from the coffee tables to the top of the bookcase. The floor was strewn with great numbers of them, with stacks forming in the recesses, leaving only a foot trail from the entryway to and around the central piece of furniture, a regulation, eight-foot, slate pool table with a red velvet top. Here, atop this most sacred spot, was built an altar worthy to be worshipped by all true believers. A mountain of beer cans, a monument to hops and barley, stacked nearly to the glass light fixture hanging from the ceiling, which in turn was filled with old beers giving off a steamed-beer vapor. Balls of rumpled clothes and pizza droppings littered the couches. The pictures on the walls, mostly prints of masterpieces, hung horribly askew, and the kitchen was a hopeless, indescribable disaster.

I made my way over to the stereo, wading through the mess where it was otherwise impassable. There I found Mr. Winter, not to my surprise, playing on an eight-track tape player Jim had torn out of an old car he totaled. It had been antique technology for ten years now. Who knew how many times it had played over and over. Jim let nothing go to waste. One time I saw his storage space, actually a thirty-foot shipping container stored on a friend's property. An aisle down the middle allowed easy access to shelves that ran the length of both sides. Every manner of mechanical device crowded these shelves from floor to ceiling. Blenders, telephones, several weed eaters, leaf blowers, food processors, dehydrators, pumps, generators, and even a mini-desalination machine. One section was dedicated to camping gear, including an entire mobile kitchen with propane everything from light to heat. There was even an assortment of twenty or so mismatched tent poles, should you ever need a tent pole. Don't get me wrong, Jungle Jim is no tinkering hobbyist collecting trash. The things that didn't work held crucial parts that he would use to bring some of those other babies back from the dead. And then, most remarkably, he would find uses for them.

I called his name a couple of times, to no avail, but when I rounded the pool table altar, I found him nearly embedded in a sofa. I had to think twice about whether a man in his drunken condition would be the right partner for a job of this enormity. But after all, who was I kidding? He was really the talent. The one who grew all those past gardens that I got credit for. Sure, I worked at it, but it had always been his talent and his determination that I had been riding on. And besides, Jim wasn't a mean drinker. Quite the opposite. In fact, he wasn't so much into drinking, he just loved to be drunk. It took a couple of minutes to rouse him from his state of complete unconsciousness. I wasn't sure what his reaction to seeing me would be. The last time I saw him, he was somewhat pissed off about my perceived lack of backbone. But when the clouds lifted, he was overjoyed to see me. "Jason Garrett, my buddy!" he said, sitting up. "Is it really you?"

Being a little overwhelmed by this unexpected reaction, I just chuckled and said, "Yeah, man, it's me."

"I can't believe it," he said, "but of course, it had to be." He put his hands on each of my shoulders. His eyes teared and, smiling, searched mine for understanding. "I knew you'd come," he said sincerely, "just when I needed you. I knew you'd come." His head sank to my chest, and he gave me a heartfelt hug. I thought I felt him crying, but before I had a chance to comfort him, he jumped to his feet, wiped his eyes, and tried to play it off like he was laughing. He picked up a half-drunk can of beer and downed it as if he was positive it was the same one he'd left off drinking before he passed out the previous night. Then he glanced just over my head and made a perfect "sky-hook" shot that saw the can land squarely in the glass of the light fixture above the pool table. "See! I've still got it! You have work for me?" he assumed.

"Well, yeah... you know... my motives aren't entirely unselfish." I was touched at his expression of trust and faith, but actually I had no idea he needed me, though I probably should have.

"It doesn't matter, boss," he said, putting on socks and shoes. "You're here right on time, no matter the motive. And I'm ready. Whether we are driving, selling, or growing. Indoor or out. I don't really care!"

"Don't you want to know how much?" I asked, pursuing him as he backed around the room looking for things.

"Naw. You've never done me wrong, boss," he said, pocketing his wallet, a small hairbrush, and a gold pocket-watch on a small chain that had belonged to his granddad—long dead and not missed, as he was a cantankerous old son of a bitch, and JJ didn't much like him.

"This is the most risk I've ever asked you to take," I said. Not wanting to assume all the responsibility, I found myself in the uncomfortable position of trying to talk him out of it.

"Okay. All right. How much?" He deftly disconnected the eight-track and placed it in a leather shoulder bag containing a dozen cassettes and had gathered a pair of jeans and two tee-shirts, which he was about to stuff in the bag, when I dropped it on him.

"A guaranteed salary of twenty grand a month..." I said, knowing I could have gotten him for ten. Without hesitating, he dropped the bag and before I could finish, "...plus bonuses," he reached for the nearest beer can and, in his best Larry Bird impression, began pretend-dribbling it around the table, dodging and faking imaginary defenders as he drove for the fixture. He put a move on me that I am sure would have faked me out of my shoes had I been in the same fantasyland as he was. Then, charging the lane, he leapt for the hoop, soaring in mid-air like a cartoon character, before slamming the container into the innocent glass fixture, shattering it to pieces and landing squarely on the beer-can altar. He tumbled backwards off the table, landing in a heap on the floor, the once-towering house of empties showering down on top of him. I wanted to laugh out loud, but as I dug him out of the pile, I was a little worried that he might have broken something. Jim never went after anything without total dedication to the cause. Unfazed by his pile-up, he brushed the beer dribble off himself and spying a nearby forty-ounce can of Colt 45, he tucked it under his arm like a Heisman trophy winner, and making his best straight-arm pose, he cut through his imaginary line of scrimmage and made for the door, breaking tackles all the way. Within seconds, the door swung shut, and he was gone. I was left with my jaw hanging open to survey the wreckage left behind. Slowly, I collected his bag of valuables, jammed in his meager threads, and backed out, taking one last mental picture before hightailing it over the cliff. What was once an upscale vacation rental was now reduced to a fixer-upper. It would need new paint and carpets. Most of the furnishings and appliances would need to be replaced, and they were going to need a truck to haul out the aluminum.

Jim's end of the money from our busted warehouse, which he had been using to pay the fifteen-hundred-a-week lease on that place, had run out a month previously, leaving the rent seriously in arrears. Now—with his landlord on the warpath and his neighbors in a froth over the endless stream of local, college-age girls flip-flopping across the lawn at all hours—was the perfect time to make a quick escape, but by the time I got back to my car, he was calmly sitting on the hood, smoking a joint in broad daylight, seemingly oblivious to the bedraggled state of his affairs. He held the joint out to me, causing my inner security alarms to go off. My eyes made a cursory check of the periphery, and I was about to turn my back on him when he said, "My laaaast joint." He smiled with the pride of a man who had survived the desert with only one sip of water to spare. "Mach 4 roaches kachink... chink ... chink," he snickered, making a sound like change falling into a cash register drawer.

He's a fool, yes, but an irresistible fool. "Gimme that," I said, laughing. "Get in the car."

*　　*　　*　　*　　*　　*　　*

The car still echoed with stories of his misadventures long after he had fallen asleep. It wasn't until spring before our hero had surfaced in Santa Cruz after a long winter hiding out. Soon after Charlie paid him his share of the busted warehouse, he popped up on the beach, where he shared his large herb stash with the locals, creating a nightly party scene from which he culled out the most innocent and the most willing. Not that the rich and beautiful didn't figure in. It's just that he desired and attracted women who really wanted it. He wasn't a braggart. It was more like he wanted to share the beauty of those tales as they rolled out one after another. Like the tale of the nineteen-year-old, Irish clog-dancer with jet black hair and bright green eyes who "doesn't even want me to fuck her, she just loves to suck dick, then smiles and walks away." Or the thirty-three-year-old, buxom, blonde massage therapist who once strapped him to her massage table and repeatedly raped him. The five-hour drive went by in a testosterone minute, with JJ sleeping the last two hours, until I shut off the engine and pulled the blanket off his head.

"Where are we?" he asked as he looked around, groggy-eyed.

"You just landed in Infinity Garden," I answered in my best Rod Serling voice.

As the elevator clicked into place one floor down, Jim finished strapping on his sidearm. Nothing much had survived his summer of debauchery, save his favorite garden clippers, which he wore in a sheath and kept sharp and as well-oiled as a marine's weapon. He knew we were headed to a big garden, but he was thrilled when the doors opened and he found Chet waiting to greet us in the anther room. He loved working for Chet. Everything was always just perfect and big time. He fussed all over Chet, saying over and over that he hadn't known this was his project and getting excited to the point of emotional, like a drunk friend who keeps saying, "I love you, man!" He was more enthusiastic about having Chet as a partner than he was when the garden revealed itself. He was not so impressed by the size of the room, as by this time he fully expected it to be huge. He simply drew his tool from its holster and went to work. Chet and I just stared with amusement for a while, then conspired between ourselves while JJ got lost in the far reaches of the garden. We could hear his alternate moans of delight and then sadness as he examined first one plant and then another. He praised the healthy ones and pruned the sickly ones, and we paid little attention until he cut down a few trees that had grown lanky and tall with wispy bud growth, sending a shock through Chet's system. "Hey, what are you doing?" he protested.

Chet knew nothing about growing pot, and Jim knew it. He handed Chet the amputated limbs and said, "You want it?" with the deadpan face of a mother administering tough love.

"But that was one of the big ones," Chet said, realizing it was already too late.

I tried to jump in and assure him. "Jim knows what he's doing."

"But can't you get anything off of it?" he whined.

Jim looked around the room and then made a sweeping gesture with his hand, as if to point out something that was obvious. Then grabbing another plant by the throat, he said, "We can't mess around with this," then he squeezed the shears like a pistol trigger and separated another victim from its stump.

Chet visibly cringed, so I figured we'd better move on. In the moms' room it continued along in the same vein. Jim, not even noticing the grandeur of the room or the size of the clone box, went right to work doctoring the cuttings and flattering the moms. The only thing he did get bubbly over was the little bed which he was so hot on you would have thought it was a suite at the Hilton. Chet and I shared a glance as Jim tested the firmness of the mattress. Chet knew Jim well from previous escapades. Although he regarded him as trustworthy and capable, two qualities he considered requisite, he felt Jim was a bit of a buffoon. A perennial underling. Someone who was not serious enough to rise to the next level. But you couldn't help but be impressed with him at times, and he was always fun to work with. In fact, his enthusiasm was contagious, and after seeing his ebullient reaction to the sleeper, Chet couldn't wait to blow his mind with the rest of the apartment.

"You think this is something?" he said with the grin of a little boy about to set off a firecracker. "Then you gotta check this out." JJ followed him back to the elevator, where he issued both of us flashlights. Once aboard with the key reinserted, we descended to level two. Approaching from the garden side this time, the room felt cold and empty, like a subterranean cave. A still, lifeless place where not even a spider would cast a web for the lack of flies. This would be a job of much deprivation, requiring a man of great willpower and sense of purpose. Or perhaps, a man nearly crazy who could fill these empty rooms with machinations of the mind. Knowing this, Chet had done his best to give us all the comforts of home. He crossed to the living quarters straight away, but, halfway through the empty room, Jim realized the implications of this second giant space. He shone the light over the stacks of boxes and, with an expectant raised eyebrow, asked, "What's this?"

"Room number two..." I said, directing my light at him. His face went ashen white as the blood drained to his penis, "...of three," I finished. It only took a moment for the realization to set in. He slipped into a blank stare as he calculated. This was roughly a three-to-four-million-dollar garden for which he would get a guaranteed quarter-mil plus a bonus. But I knew that before he started to wonder why he was only getting a twelfth of the gross, he would get lost in the fantasy of running the largest indoor grow in the world. As I pulled him toward the door to our new home, he scanned the various piles of boxes, purring over each in turn. Now he was sufficiently enthralled in delusions of grandeur for me to let loose the catch.

"So, now that you have seen the enormity of our job," I tried to ease the bad news out slowly, "I know you'll understand why it is necessary that we...live here full-time."

Anyone who has ever done it knows it to be true, that living in an indoor garden for long stretches can wreck you, both physically and mentally. The stress dances across your nervous system like a tap-dancing hippo on a pane of glass. Jim knew this, and, even with such a great temptation, he would have to think twice before sacrificing his life to his livelihood. "Naw, we won't have to do that!" he exclaimed with a worried half-chuckle. "We can do this in three or four days a week apiece." He looked around again. "Maybe five."

"I'm afraid so, son," I said in a fatherly way, putting my arm around his shoulder just as we got to the door of the apartment. He knew in his heart that I was right. "This calls for absolute devotion to the cause, including top-flight security precautions."

"But..." He was about to continue his protestations when I opened the door and interrupted.

"Just think of it this way," I said as I guided him into the Cannabis Condo, "you get a thousand dollars for every day you spend... in here." JJ went goo-goo-eyed as he took in the glory of this home. Velvet window treatments turned solid cement walls into fantastic false windows. Plush carpets and sumptuous furniture invited you to take off your shoes and fall in. All in soft dark colors of deep blue, violet, and maroon to offset the bright light of the workspace. But when he saw the entertainment center with all the video games he liked attached to that huge screen and wired through an excellent sound system, he was beside himself with orgasmic delight. He retrieved the master remote from its place on the armrest of the recliner, like Excalibur from the stone, then flitted about the room from one toy to the next, trying them all out at once. Chet looked at me as would one fisherman to another, with admiration for the way I had set the hook and then delivered my catch to the deck. All that was left to do was shake on it, but we practically had to wrestle Jimmy Boy into the chair to talk business. He had the spice channel dialed up on the big screen and was completely absorbed by a giant man eating pussy, when we asked him if he wanted in. He just laughed, insanely, and said in a voice that was half-whisper and half-growl, "Are you fuckin' kidding!?"

# CHAPTER 13

I had already instructed Drake to pick out ten healthy cuttings to serve as our new moms at the mill, but now, determined to make that building flush with heavy, green Elvis plants in record time, I made him a deal impossible to refuse. I insisted that he root three hundred cuttings for me in the next three weeks and again for each of the two following three-week periods. He resisted. This would be an incredible amount of work and would "surely cripple" his own garden.

I reminded him that I had built that garden for him, twice! And that he hadn't had great luck running it without me. Nevertheless, I promised to compensate him well for both his work and his loss. If he would promise to deliver what I needed, even to the detriment of his own project, I would pay him fifty bucks a cutting—twice the going rate—and walk away from any claims I had on his crop, while continuing to troubleshoot for him when necessary. This would pay for his loss in full in one cycle, while he would retain my twenty-five percent in perpetuity.

Once he fully understood, he readily agreed, and we immediately set out to fill the clone box. In the first three weeks, we were only able to cut half our needs, but in the meantime, our ten mothers came into their own. After six weeks we had a full complement of rooted cuttings for the first two floors of the mill and two plants per light for Drake's bloom room. He would still get a full crop, but it would take three weeks longer than usual to fill the space with bigger trees. In the past, we had tried every new garden toy that came out. Rockwool, an asbestos-type medium, allowed us to recirculate and recapture expensive nutrient-rich water, and $CO_2$ emitters to promote growth, with controllers that simultaneously shut off the ventilation fans to retain the $CO_2$. We had lights that moved on tracks, cloning hormone to enhance root growth, huge ozone generators to eliminate the smell, and so on. But this time, even though it was a much bigger project than any before, we intended to get much closer to the ground. Dirt and different composts and guanos, and natural soluble fertilizers used sparingly, then down the drain. Not using recaptured water helped prevent salt build-up, and alternating sodium and halide lights allowed for the largest possible spectrum of light. Basically, the idea was back to fundamentals. Dirt, light, water. Just like the old days, save the clones.

By the time I brought in the first three-hundred beauties, the second floor was primed and waiting. While we waited for Chet to procure the supplies for floor three, something he was very good at, we completely remodeled the first floor to fit our new scheme, including the remaining ten lights of mature tops, which we harvested that night. Over the next two days, we filled the second floor to capacity, as well as thirty lights upstairs. After a lot of hard work, we were at half-capacity and running green. Chet was very pleased when he returned to find the place had come to life. He praised us all thoroughly and treated us to a box full of edible delicacies and fine drink. We watched rented movies and got high all night, and Chet hung out like one of the boys, something he was normally uncomfortable doing. He even smoked right along with us until he passed out on the comfy couch.

Jim and I awoke simultaneously the next morning, him on the lush king-size and me on the pull-out sofa-bed. He smiled at me with dreamy-eyed satisfaction, taking a quiet moment to appreciate the splendor of his new home. It was so nicely appointed one would think an interior decorator had done it. With all matching furniture and color scheme, the window treatments complementing the bedspread, and even a wide array of interesting knick-knacks and art pieces to occupy a wandering mind. Jim sat up and suddenly became very animated, "This is the nicest house I have ever had!" he exclaimed, jumping to his feet, hopping around on the bed, and singing, "We all live in a green pot machine... a green pot machine... a green pot machine."

"Except for a few drawbacks," I said. He shot me a disappointed look, annoyed by my habit of throwing cold water on his flame. "No windows and no women."

That stunned him. He stopped jumping for a moment and accusingly said, "Oh, why you want to do that?" He shook his head as if trying to get me out of it and said aloud to himself, "No!" Then waving me off, he started jumping again and making up songs like a little kid. "And we live a life of ease... in our green pot machine." Having learned my lesson, I shut up, and he went on for a few minutes until we both started to feel a deep vibration in the walls. Jimmy stopped, and we held our collective breath trying to get a bead on it, as the adrenal gland went to work. Then, like firemen responding to a five-alarm blaze, we leapt into our clothes and dashed up the stairs. As we reached the top of the stairwell, the vibration turned to a loud noise, and by carefully peeking through a crack between the double doors, we identified it as a big truck that had backed up to our loading dock. We could hear Chet barking out directions, but we didn't want anyone to see us, so we waited at the top of the stairwell for about five minutes until the truck pulled out. We emerged to find Chet beaming with pride and grinning from side to side. Next to him on the dock were five pallets of boxes nicely wrapped in sheet plastic. "Here you go," he said triumphantly. "All the equipment for the third floor, plus every other item on your list." It wasn't easy to procure large orders of grow supplies. The cops were watching the light stores, and ever since Operation Green Merchant—when the cops seized the credit card receipts and phone records of many of the major distributors—not to mention shutting down Sinsemilla Tips magazine, we growers had gotten extremely leery of shopping trips. Chet used cut-outs, a CIA term for an operative who insulates him from danger, who in turn uses his own cut-outs, so that the person who bought that truckload of illicit supplies didn't even know Chet. Then before it came to us, the stuff was shifted from one storage facility to another until he was sure no one was tracking it. I took some time to praise him for this trick, but JJ went straight to the pallets and began skinning the plastic with his clippers. He had the focus of a bird dog, and once he locked on the scent, there was no calling him off. Chet announced that he was taking off, but Jim was already in a trance, and nobody could break the spell. Before leaving, Chet instructed me to take our meager harvest, maybe seven pounds dry, to the trim-and-dry set-up in a house in a small farm town in the San Joaquin Valley, halfway back to the city. I would have to go in blind, never having been there before and not knowing the people who would meet me. Just explicit directions, a mobile phone with their beeper number, and a garage-door opener. This was uncomfortable, though common when working with Chet. But the thing that really unnerved me was another sealed, heavy box that he gave me with more instructions for delivery to a guy named Ramón—whom I didn't know—at an open-air meeting in a parking lot in downtown Oakland. This time I couldn't resist the urge to peek inside, and I was completely astonished at what I saw. Thirty or more assorted boxes of Girl Scout cookies! What possible reason could he have for having me deliver cookies to these suspicious characters, disguised as a marine?! The question was still spinning around my head when I met Ramón, a small, wiry Latino with an overly friendly grin that spoke in badly broken English, and his two big body guards with bulging armpits. But why shouldn't he be friendly? I just gave him a big box of cookies! Once again, I suppressed the voice of my Narrator saying, "Don't do it!" and trusted Chet's wisdom, with prayers that it wouldn't come back to haunt me.

# CHAPTER 14

I rolled into the town at dusk in a "company" van purchased solely for the purpose of hauling the harvest. As instructed I made several tiring anti-surveillance maneuvers, which were, as I predicted, totally unnecessary. But Chet had insisted, so I played along. I was supposed to drive straight into the garage, nonstop, once I reached the neighborhood, but the hairs on the back of my neck wouldn't let me obey that order. It was unfamiliar territory, so I cruised by once to check it out. My destination was a large, three-story farmhouse with a pointed roof and three chimneys. The beautiful, old Victorian, quite ornate in its day, once sat on a large parcel of land on the outskirts of town, but it had now surrendered all but an acre to the town that had grown to engulf it. There were no lights on yet and no sign anyone would be there to receive me, except for an unfamiliar, forest-green Ford F250 pick-up with camper shell parked to the side of the garage. One trip around the block to check for suspicious characters or vehicles, then, with my heart racing—just as I lined up on the driveway ready to make a clean entry—I dropped the remote opener on the floor under my legs. The Narrator screamed, "Fumble!" as I negotiated with the steering wheel for access to the floor. Forced to come to an abrupt halt in front of the garage, I exhaled mightily in an attempt to contort myself into the angle necessary to retrieve the fallen key. Ironically, I was in this kiss-your-ass-good-bye position when I heard a revving of engines and squealing of tires that I usually associate with pouncing DEA agents. It sent my body surfing through a cocktail of mind chemicals—adrenaline, endorphins, and dopamine—that, combined with lack of oxygen, nearly caused me to swoon. Just as I was being sucked into the spinning darkness of a cyclone, I heard the garage door engage and jerked myself into an upright position, hitting my head on the turn signal and activating the windshield wipers. By now, the cars had disappeared around the bend—probably a couple of teenagers out racing around—leaving me alone in a screaming paranoid sweat. There I was, in a still, calm neighborhood, with my heart pumping and my head pounding in time to the turn signal and the wipers slapping away at full tilt. I casually shut them off and eased the van into the garage. The door closed tightly behind, leaving me in the dim light of the automatic opener until very bright interior fluorescents signaled the entrance of my host.

I braced myself for the arrival of this uncomfortable moment. Probably some geeky East Coast spook who would want to chat me up. Some kind of efficiency expert I'd have nothing in common with. I resolved to make my delivery, take a good look around, impress upon this guy the importance of hash collection, and then break out of this sardine can. That is, until Carlotta Micos came slinking through the door, blowing me over like a dried-up fan leaf. I had been deceived! Played! Chet had usurped my whole crew and cut me out of the middle. This was something I wouldn't put past him, or even hold against him. After all, I was getting paid. But Charlie? Scheming and plotting against her man? She must have been in on it from the start, and it looked like she was feeling pretty guilty, 'cause she was only wearing a baby-blue, lace halter top with matching short-short skirt that did little to obscure her ample behind—and a pout. There must have been matching panties to go with the ensemble, but when she whirled around and skipped out with her best betcha-can't-catch-me look, she let it be known she hadn't bothered with them.

Now, I can get as angry as the next guy when a woman plays me for a fool, and I'd just been played by this one. It came to me as clear as a lightning flash the instant I saw that face. That lovely, tantalizing face. And if she thought she could use her feminine wiles and that body... ooooh, that body. Carlotta was indeed a beautiful woman. And when I say woman, I don't mean the bouncy, giggling hard-bodies one might see in fantasies, but a sultry, seductive, mature woman. With the sexual prowess to possess a man, mind and body... But not me! I tried to steel myself against her power, but clearly my self-righteous anger was no match for her forces of nature, and she was able to turn the little soldier against me with a single look. My intention had been to carefully case the joint. I wanted to check their security precautions, the facilities, the quality of their work, and hash collection, but it turned into more of a wild pussy hunt. Even my Narrator was consumed by the passion as I stalked from room to room, not even noticing the spacious environs and grand ceilings as my dick divined the way. Up a wide, wooden staircase with ornate handrails that faced the front entranceway. Invading each of the bedrooms that lined either side of a broad hall, with no consideration of who I might find. First one, then another, like a rampaging Hun, until I came to the master bedroom, its door locked in a feeble attempt to bar my entry. But it was too late. I had already grown the horns of a Viking, and though I could have opened the door with a butter knife, I opted instead to go with the mood and put my foot through it, slamming it against an inside wall and splintering the jam to bits. Charlie stopped laughing for a moment, and all I could hear was our breathing. She lay sprawled out on a laced, four-poster bed, up against a brace of pillows gazing into my eyes with a look of fear mixed with lust. I paused a little too long. "Well?" she said.

"You lied to me," I said, a little out of breath.

"I did not!" she responded indignantly.

"You misled." I tried to be pissed.

She reached back over her head with both hands, grasping the headboard behind her, causing the lace halter to ride up exposing the underside of her breasts down to her waist, where the mini-skirt surrendered any pretense of modesty. She was slightly turned on one hip, barely revealing the object of my desire. "Was that so bad?" she teased. She caught me heroically trying to avert my eyes from her patch and stared into them with burning intensity, daring me not to look, as she slowly and purposely let her legs fall wide open. Now, I've been schooled not to stare at a lady, but in this instance, I felt it would be impolite not to. She watched me, excited by her power, as her hand trailed across her thigh and brushed her blond mound. Then with a very serious look she said, "Come and get it!"

While she watched impatiently, I stripped off my clothes and approached the bed, never taking my eyes off what I wanted. She backed up against the headboard like cornered prey and tried to shield her deliciousness with her hands and arms. I parted the curtains and kept coming. She curled her knees into the fetal position just as I fell on her. I tried to kiss her, but she turned her head away slightly, forcing me to chase her with my lips, almost pinning her down before she relented and kissed me back the way a starving man would attack a juicy steak. Then she pulled back like it was something she really needed but had to resist. She momentarily escaped my grasp, and, turning her backside to me, tried to burrow into the pillows. Now, I'm not a violent man, and I always try to be the gentlest of lovers—a more-better tongue-lasher than cocksman—but by now my dick had become a battering ram, and raising that ass up in my face was like waving a red flag in front of a bull. I seized her hips and pulled her to me. I tried, momentarily, to fondle her, but she resisted, grunting, "No," and pushing herself up against me. She had seen the condition of the pole, and like a kid who builds a huge ice cream cone, she was ready to devour her creation. I poked around a little, trying unnecessarily to heighten her excitement, but she would have none of that. Forcing me to enter her fully on the first stroke, she bucked wildly, driving me into a frenzy. I crushed her into the bed and pounded her mercilessly, as she squirmed and clawed the sheets, making a halfhearted attempt at escape. I had never before fucked anyone who was trying to get away, and it was a little disconcerting because I didn't want to hurt her, but every few minutes her grunting turned to pleased laughter as she saw the condition I was in. I lasted longer than ever before, making her alternately very serious, then near giddy, time and again, until we were both spent and collapsed into a hug that was more like a Celtic knot, for the longest time.

After a while, hunger got the best of us, so we made for the kitchen, and after scarfing up several boxes of leftover Chinese food, she showed me around the place. It seemed perfectly secure. No one would ever suspect what was going on there. Even the interior showed no signs of the operation—no scissors or telltale leaf lying around. Of course, there were no plants giving away the secret with their smell, but Charlie maintained that they had that problem solved. A narrow interior door in the second floor hallway led to a thin stairway that climbed steeply into the attic. Tina Wilson and a younger lady I hadn't met appeared with the bags of harvest they had retrieved from the van and, asking no help from me, lugged them up into the drying room. It was a vast, raw space crudely floored with ply board, but otherwise uninsulated. The apex of the house was a good eight feet overhead, but sloped away pyramid-like on four sides all the way to the floor. Because of the angle of the roof, strings for hanging the branches could be placed relatively close together, maximizing space. Several hours after nightfall, it was still warm from the heat of the day, and a few requisite space heaters would take over after that. A one-inch gap under the roof's overhang ran the circumference of the room, providing intake at floor level for one exhaust port. It had a large piece of ducting attached to it for mixing in ozone, and it vented the entire room through the roof, thirty-five feet above ground and forty feet from the street.

"I figure it will hold fifty pounds," she said, surveying her work with her hands on her hips. "Any more will have to go on these racks." Two-by-eight mesh frames lined the edges of the room. "But most of the big buds will hang."

Nothing had been placed under the screens to catch the falling trichomes, which brought up another subject. "What about hash collection?" I asked.

"What about it?" she replied.

"Chet wants you to make a supreme effort to collect and clean as much as you can."

"He didn't mention it to me," she said, trying to get out of the extra work.

"Well, he will," I said, a little miffed that he hadn't.

"That's a pain in the neck," she whined, "especially on this scale."

"Yer' gettin' paid, aren't you?" I quipped.

"Well, if Chet insists." I knew she would have to do it for the boss, if not for me.

It seemed he was calling the shots now, but I had no idea how much until a few hours later when I was in the bedroom getting ready to leave. The ash on the joint I was smoking was getting long, and in my search for a place to flick it, I came across something unexpected and unwelcome. The ashtray I found under the bed was soiled with a single cigarette butt. An unmistakable, filterless Gauloises that could have been left in my honey's bedroom by no one other than my mentor, Chester Hawthorne.

*    *    *    *    *    *    *

The first full room we harvested grossed $210,000 worth of very high-quality herb. It was slightly under my quota, but no one would complain about that start. I was capable of squeezing more than a pound per light out of there, but Chet got an idea of what was to come. He was very pleased and congratulatory—until he had to cut two-hundred grand off the top for Jimmy and me. I immediately placed my share into a secret panel I'd been working on in the Mobile Hilton. He got a good chuckle when I described my surprise at finding my whole crew at the T&D, but we never spoke about him boffing my old lady for me. I guess he figured I didn't know, and I didn't really want to go there anyway. Charlie and I didn't have any spoken exclusivity to each other, even though sleeping with my partner was kind of cheesy. But a woman like her desired a man of great power. And Chet? Who could blame him for wanting her? The thought of them sitting in bed and plotting against me was irksome, but I wasn't as mad as I thought I should be. Before I left her bedroom that day, I put the ashtray with my roach and the offending butt on the nightstand for her to find. I went straight back to the mill and got drunk with JJ and Patrick, drowning my sorrows in a half-case of Hamm's that Chet kept fully stocked in the fridge, though he found it distasteful. Jim got good and soused, and, insisting on trying out ancient hash-gathering techniques, he stripped and ran through the garden, rubbing up against the plants. He frolicked up and down the aisles for a time, while Patrick and I laughed hysterically at the sight. But the experiment was a failure, as no hash was collected, and sank from comedy to tragedy when Jim awoke the next day buck naked and stuck to the leather loveseat he'd passed out on. After prying him loose with a healthy application of salad oil, we went straight to work on the third floor. It went very fast, giving us time off before the next round of harvesting, planting, transplanting and cloning, so Jim prepared to make his first escape into the world in ten weeks. He tried like hell to get me to go, but I was feeling sorry for myself, and I knew I couldn't keep up with him.

Any doubts I had were demolished after he took his "pregame" shower and returned to the living room wearing just a pair of socks and a towel wrapped around his head, like my mom used to do. I had heard him hollering at someone—really cursing 'em out—but I didn't know who it could be until he emerged with a giraffe's neck of a hard-on and a twelve-inch wooden ruler, with which he proceeded to beat the aforementioned boner rather severely. Whack. Whack. Down came the measuring stick, causing him to hop a bit. "C'mon, you bitch!" Whack... hop..."Get up there, or I'll beat you into shape." Whack... whack... hop... hop. Then he started to talk real sweetly to it like a man who'd just beaten his wife. "Oh, c'mon now, baby, you know I love you. I didn't mean it... but you gotta be tough." Whack... "You gotta be strong." Whack...whack... "cause you got work to do." I couldn't stop laughing, which only incited him more. I felt sorry for the girl who was going to run into that thing.

We completed the first cycle in four months from day one. The three rooms together grossed seven-hundred-thousand bucks. We were rolling in it, and from there on out, it would keep rolling at three-hundred-and-fifty grand a month. The three of us got into a routine that allowed not only for sanity, but for regular days off and vacations when necessary. The rest of the time, we stayed under house arrest. It was hardship duty, but at $83,333 a month, I could take it. Jim handled the T&D deliveries for that cycle, but I took over after that. It had been four months since I had seen Charlie, and though we hadn't talked about it, we both knew things would never be the same.

She wanted me to get angry with her and maybe yell a little, so she could be defensive and I'd be the bad guy. I should have, but, being the wimp I am, I tried to remain unaffected. That just pissed her off more, causing her to go into a tirade about how it was all my fault and how, I couldn't express my feelings, and she never said she wanted to marry me, dadah, dadah, dadah. As if to prove her right, I refused to lose my cool, let alone fight back. I just put on a we-both-know-you're-full-of-shit look and blew her a kiss when I left. Besides pleasantries, I only spoke to her to reinforce the hash directive. She threatened that if I wanted any hash collected, I'd damn well better collect it myself! I knew it was too much guilt for her to bear. She would have to spread out the pain, so I was prepared for a storm, though I didn't expect that kind of onslaught. She was still fuming when I pulled out. I had learned long ago that if you can't win, change the game, and since I wasn't going to have my woman, at least by not getting upset about it I could win my dignity back. It went on like that for a full year before things mellowed to cordial, and by that time, Chet had just about moved in. But my million-and-a-half bucks in cash were helping me get over it. Over the first twelve months, we pulled out fifteen rooms, eleven-hundred-and-fifty pounds. At one point, nearly two pounds average per light. After a second year, we were all floating on a sea of cash with no end in sight. With bonuses, after two and a half years, I had made close to three million bucks, and I had no safe place to put it, so I continued to pack the Hilton with bundles of cash and blocks of Elvis hash until they were stuffed. After all, who can you trust with even half a mil in cash? I passed the majority of my bonuses on to Jim, who had really put his heart into his work and was nearing a million and a half himself. I didn't know how much Patrick was making. In spite of his bellyaching, I'm sure it was considerable. Neither did I know what Pat's father's end was, though he must have been paid. Charlie was crying some about coming up on the short end of the stick. Though she made great money for a trimmer, she worked hard running a very important part of the project and probably should have made more. Chet allowed three-hundred dollars a pound for trimming and drying. Fifty bucks covered all the expenses. One-fifty for the trimmer, then with Charlie doing about five hundred of them, leaving a hundred per for running the show. After more than two years, she had earned $260,000 for managing and about $75,000 for her scissor work. With the rest of us getting rich, well-off just wasn't enough for her. But I didn't have much of an ear for it. If she needed more, she could go to the boss. I didn't know his overhead, but, by my figuring, he had to have cleared at least $6,000,000.

# CHAPTER 15

You would have thought we were planning the overthrow of the government, the way they rammed through door of the garage with a thunderous crash that rousted me from my early-morning slumber, even though it was two floors overhead. My heart was racing as though I was waking from a bad dream, but I knew this time it was real. It only took another instant for them to reach the double doors atop the stairs, but in that moment, I had time to consider everything that had led up to that point and all that was likely to come. I even had time to wonder if Patrick, who was sleeping in the kitchen above me, knew he was about to go down, but in the last two years I had acquired a distaste for his sickly sweet, self-ingratiating ways. They removed the upstairs doors from their hinges in two seconds flat, and I could hear several voices shouting commands in the mom's room above me. But by the time they busted into the apartment, I had already scurried out through the second-floor garden and anteroom and shut myself into the elevator with only a handful of clothes and my boots. There was nowhere to go, but I was running on instinct now. I unlocked the lift and hurriedly put on my clothes as it lowered to the third floor. No one seemed to notice, and I was left in quiet darkness for an exaggerated moment before panic set in and I started climbing the walls of my mind looking for a way out. But my Narrator was already calmly examining the choices. There were only three ways out of that concrete tomb. The stairs and elevator were useless at this point, leaving only the exhaust vent to the chimney stack, and as improbable as that seemed, a drowning man will clutch at anything to stay afloat. So I seized one of the steel blades on the fan and, with super-human strength, bent it far enough out that I could shimmy through the opening into the shaft beyond. It took quite a few minutes for them to get down there, and when they finally entered, they did so cautiously, as the lights were out. This gave me just enough time to pull the blade back into position before they searched the room with flashlights. I tried to assess my position without breathing, as the cops were right on the other side of the wall. The shaft was a rectangle about four-by-six, of the same concrete construction as the rest of the building. No tin ducting, just a cement column narrowing slightly as it rose into the darkness. The only light emanated from the two fans above. Brighter on the first floor because the grow lights were on and less so on the second, where they must have turned on the work lights. The six or more cops on my floor were surprised by the loud popping of two ballasts that ignited right beside them. Turning on the lights had to be staggered to prevent the electrical surge that would occur if too many were turned on at once. But the cops, not knowing this, were understandably unnerved by the repetitive popping in the far parts of the room, accompanied by the dim light cast by bulbs in the warm-up mode. I, however, knew exactly what was going on—sixty thousand watts to be precise—and if I was to remain undiscovered, I could not stay in that vulnerable position. I searched the walls with my fingers and, to my delight, found a piece of rebar protruding out about two inches at a height of about two feet from the floor. I fumbled in the darkness trying to find a hand-hold higher up, while the cops had their guns drawn not three feet away. Finding another rebar end at about six feet up, I began to scale the interior of the shaft, pausing only for a moment to peek through the fan to marvel for the last time at the magnificence of my garden in the rising electric sun. This level was in full bloom, with swollen bract from the ceiling to the floor and wall to wall and ready to harvest. It was a brilliant testament to the depth of our dedication, to our hard work and ingenuity. But moreover, it was a living expression of our desire to be free, both literally and figuratively. But this time, they would get it all.

Luckily, Jungle Jim was on a weekend pass and would not be able to perform his usual misguided heroics. He spotted the caravan of police vehicles coming through the town where he had stopped for gas, and followed them down the road a piece before stashing the company van on a fire road near the mill. Continuing on foot through the surrounding forest adjacent to our garage, he hunkered down and helplessly watched the assault. Half-a-dozen sheriffs' cars, a van, two unmarked units holding four guys with D.E.A. jackets and side-arms, as well as a special weapons team wearing bulletproof vests and carrying automatic weapons. Our triple-locked door was no match for the battering ram, and in seconds, a flood of agents washed into the mill. There was nothing Jim could do, but he stayed and looked on for hours, fearing discovery only one time. Several deputies made a quick search of the woods, but he had already dug in under a fallen pine tree by then and camouflaged himself with the scotch broom that grew on the edge of the forest.

I had managed to climb to the second floor by using my rebar grips and wedging myself between the walls just before those blazing halides illuminated my slightly shielded hiding spot. One officer tried to peek behind the fan, but I was already over his head. They brought Patrick, handcuffed, into the first-floor bloom room and sat him in a folding chair just outside the moms' room. I could clearly hear them talking just above me, and although it was risky to move, I couldn't resist the urge to get close enough to see. As quietly as possible, I dislodged myself and, using brute force more than agility, lifted myself another ten feet to a perch behind the first floor exhaust fan where I could clearly see Pat not fifteen feet away. The way he was facing me looked almost staged, but I was invisible in the shadows. One of the plain-clothed, D.E.A. types began the questioning, "What's yer' name, son?" he asked.

"Patrick."

"Patrick what?" The cop jammed him up for his last name really quick, and Patrick answered from rote.

"Halston."

"Patrick Halston, my name is Agent Bill Kassen of the D.E.A. and from this point on, I have complete control over your future." He fancied himself a classy, southern-mannered super-sleuth and looked the part, with highly tailored clothes and a smallish bowler-type hat over blond hair and a matching mustache trimmed precisely to the corners of his mouth. But behind the facade he was just a crude shit-kicker in a good suit.

One of the other agents spoke up. "Are you any relation to the Leonard Halston who owns the mill?"

"He's my pop," Patrick answered regretfully.

"Well, this is some kind of operation you've got here," Kassen said patronizingly. "I don't think we've ever seen one this big. Or this sophisticated." Patrick looked terrified, but he kept his mouth shut, and I remained hopeful. I was even comfortable lodged into my crevice.

"Where're yer' partners?" the federal cop asked in that authoritative tone I hate.

"Whadaya' mean?" Patrick tried to play dumb.

"Yer' not going ta' tell me ya' built all this yerself." Now in a disgusted tone.

"Well... no... I'm only a mechanic here. I just did some construction."

"I see," the cop said, now with an understanding tone. "This isn't your grow. You just did a little construction work here, right?"

"Well, ya' know, plumbing and electrical. That kind of stuff." Pat hoped he had a compassionate cop here.

"Right, right. You didn't plant anything or sell any of the crop or anything like that." This wasn't the first time this cop had interviewed a suspect, and he knew this guy was a pushover.

"No! No way, offIcer,"

"So tell me, where're yer' partners?" Kassen asked again.

"I don't know." Pat was still trying to avoid the questions when he should have kept his mouth shut.

"What're their names?" the cop pursued.

"Well," he paused, and I thought he would give it up right there. "I don't really even know."

The pig got loud and right in his face. "You know yer' gonna' go to prison fer' twenty to thirty? I guess yer' the kingpin here! Is that what yer telling me?"

"No!" His voice was starting to waver along with his backbone.

"Well, if I don't get some names from you purty' quick, I'm going ta' have ta' assume yer' the boss, and you'll have ta' carry the whole load. Don't matter ta' me. Jus' another day on the job." Patrick didn't answer, so the cop pulled out the stops. "Or maybe you'd like it if I go up an' bust yer' daddy."

"Chet!" he blurted out. It was as easy as that. That was all it took to get him to turn on his friend.

"Chet? Chet what?" The cop reeled him in.

"I'm not even sure." It was too late to scramble.

"Son, I'm gonna find out everything I wanna know anyway. But whoever it is that helps me is gonna get a break on this deal. Now I know that you aren't the top dog around here, and I don't understand why you would take the fall fer' him. You seem like a good kid, but if you wannna' cut yer' own throat, makes no matter to me."

"Chester Hawthorne," he broke.

"Chester Hawthorne, you said?" Kassen repeated.

"Yeah, and two other guys. Jason Garrett and some dude, name of Jim. I don't know his last name, and that's the truth."

I just about fell out of my tree. The son of a bitch didn't even try. Why is it, no matter how many times you tell someone to say nothing to the police, they invariably try to talk themselves out of it? It never works! These cops are slugs, and they are experts at taking advantage of the stupid. Now they had my name and someone to testify against me, but I'd been in similar circumstances before and survived, so I still entertained delusions of escape. I watched as they took a video statement, which nearly made me sick to my stomach. Patrick opened with the ease of a luggage lock, telling them everything they wanted to know in great detail. He gave them descriptions of each of us, including when and where he had met us. He told them how long we'd been running and about how much we'd harvested. He even revealed that I had slept in the building that night. He gave up all our phone numbers and codes, and even tried to get Chet on the phone while they listened. If he could get Chet to implicate himself over the wire, they promised, it would go easier on him. They flipped him like a flapjack, but there was a whole lot they didn't get. He knew absolutely nothing about the trim-and-dry or sales operations. In both areas Chet had insisted on complete autonomy, so Charlie was safe, and he knew precious few facts about Jim. I wasn't so lucky. He had a lot more history on me—my last name, vehicle descriptions, a previous address, and a short history of my dope-dealing past. He lined me up like a field goal and kicked me right between the posts. There was nothing I could do. Just sit there in silent horror as he splayed me open. I wanted to reach through that fan and choke the squealing puss out of him, and he was almost that close, but I had to contain my animus, promising myself I'd kill him slowly for his betrayal.

After they had wrung him dry, they thanked him for cooperating and reiterated their promises to help him, then dragged him off to jail in chains. As they were pulling out of the building, two sheriffs' deputies lingered behind, and when they were alone, or so they thought, they began to fill a garbage bag with wet tops, admiring the high quality and celebrating their good fortune. I remained crammed into my sanctuary, listening to them argue over how much was enough. The one who just wanted to fill a bag and get out won out over the more greedy officer, who would have been more thorough. When they were gone, an eerie quiet remained. Work lights and doors were left carelessly open, something you'd never see in an indoor garden, as light leaks would ruin the crop, and a clean breeze blew through the once-still rooms as the fans sucked outside air down the stairs.

\* \* \* \* \* \* \*

Jim watched as they put Patrick into the paddy wagon and retreated. Except one sheriff's cruiser that went around to the mill's office, where it remained for an hour or so before Jim watched it leave through the front gate. Once again they had sealed the demolished entry with only plastic police tape, and left. The Mobile Hilton was the only vehicle left behind, so Jim knew I must be in there. There were no traces of cops anywhere, and he desperately wanted to come get me, but before he came out of hiding, a county truck pulled in, and a crew of four workers filed into the garage.

\* \* \* \* \* \* \*

As soon as I was alone, I pulled myself up the remaining ten feet to ground level. I positioned myself just inside a wire grate that vented the garage at floor level. It was about two-feet square, right next to the unhinged stairwell door, and I was just about to kick through it when the workers pulled up. It would be a solid four hours of dangling in the shaft before they left.

They went to work on the ripe third floor first, mercilessly ripping out the swollen plants and smashing them into trash bags. The immature floors followed suit, as they cleared all the plants out first, then turned to the nuts and bolts of dismantling the rooms. My whole body was one solid cramp by the time they finished stuffing the van and left. This time I could wait no more. I put my foot through the screen right up to the knee, slamming it into the quiet garage. Then I quickly pulled myself through head first. When my legs cleared the hole, I rolled away and lay exhausted in the sawdust. For a few minutes, I allowed my muscles to relax, feeling the tension subside one level at a time. Just as I would get one muscle to relax, I'd realize there was another level of tension under it. My mind cleared as the waves of relaxation washed over me, momentarily replacing the fear, but, having got this far, it was no time to let down. I jumped to my feet and jogged to each of the three roll-up doors in turn, trying to get a look outside. From under the third roll-up, I could see the right-side wheels of the Hilton right outside, all by herself, packed to the hilt with my earnings. I strained for a better look but couldn't see what was in the periphery, so I went to the broken door. It had been left ajar, as it would no longer close, but I was still unable to see anything, so I cracked it open a little farther, craning my neck through the opening to peek at the yard.

*    *    *    *    *    *    *

Jim watched carefully as the workers cleared our home. He almost couldn't contain his anger as they withdrew bag after bag of his last harvest, but he calmed down some when they turned to the equipment. Taking his aggression out on his hiding tree, he cut a notch with his clippers for every light and every ballast they removed. They worked very hard the entire time and were very efficient, but that truck just wasn't big enough for the whole job, and, by his count, they only managed to fit seventy-five systems on the first load. They took off around five o'clock in the afternoon. By then, he had resolved to wait until dark and, if no one returned, he'd go in and check it out. There could possibly be some herb left. He had just settled back into his foxhole when he heard the front door creak open, so he popped his head out right in time to see me peeking around the base of the broken door. He came out of his hole a bit and tried to signal me with his hands but was afraid to reveal himself. Although he had not seen any agents in a while, it was not safe to assume they weren't around. He crawled on his belly to the very edge of the gravel and tried desperately to get my attention without giving himself away. But he wasn't the only one who had heard the door creak. Agent William Kassen was also a man with patience and, with his partner, had also waited in the shadows for his prey. He knew that I had slept there, and, unless I had managed to scurry out on foot unnoticed, I still had to be there. He spied around the corner of the building, anticipating my next move and giving away his position to Jim, who, he was unaware, was looking on from the tree line. Jim was horrified when he saw Kassen, gun out, closing in on his friend. He picked up some pebbles and was about to throw them my way to raise an alarm, but it was too late.

\*   \*   \*   \*   \*   \*   \*

I couldn't see a damn thing moving out there. They hadn't towed my van yet, but stranger things have happened. Dusk was just falling, and I had been trapped in that shaft for so long I just had to make a break for it. I stood up, and, opening the door still more, I slipped sideways through the passage into the open. I stayed there for an instant, checking further for anything moving. I had no idea Jim was

CHAPTER 15

there, only thirty yards away, nearly having a seizure as he watched Kassen inch closer. Then, like a scared jackrabbit, I made my move. With keys in hand, I bolted for the van. It was only forty feet away, but I reached a full-sprint in half that distance. I made right for the driver's door, and, just as I reached for the handle, Kassen rounded the rear and nailed me. He didn't shout "freeze" the way they do on TV. Instead he spoke softly through his teeth, "Now where in hell you think yer' goin', you little fuck?!" Now, I'm not really a little guy, but Kassen made me look like one. At six-four, he stood several inches taller than I, and at two-fifty, he outweighed me by seventy pounds. I had nearly made it to freedom, and my disappointment made me lose my manners. "Shit!" I said, kicking the door.

Taking that as a threatening gesture, he changed his gun to his left hand and slugged me right in the gut. Then, grabbing me by the collar with the gun hand and taking my wrist in his other, he whipped me around and slammed me into the van. Almost simultaneously, he cuffed my right hand, kneed me in the back—forcing me up against the van—cuffed my left hand, and backed off like a rodeo cowboy who had just roped and hogtied a calf in record time. This left me off balance to fall face-first into the ground. By the time Agent Nolan came around the front end of the van, Kassen had his foot on my neck, like the king of the mountain, pressing my cheek into the gravel. I screamed in pain as Kassen said, "I got this punk."

Nolan put his hand on Kassen's arm and said, "Okay. Okay. Ease up. Ease up on 'im, Kase," talking Kassen down as if he were some kind of psychotic.

Kassen kicked me a good one right in the ribs as he muttered, "Little shit! Little fucking punk!"

*　*　*　*　*　*　*

Jim slithered back into his hole and covered his head with his arms, trying to protect himself from the pain of watching those pigs throwing his brother into their car to be hauled off to jail. He lay there until way after dark. Then, when he was sure it was clear, he raced from the woods right through the police tape into our busted project. Once inside, he knew he had the whole place to himself, but his adrenaline was still pumping as if someone were chasing him. He made right for the third-floor bloom room. He found it destroyed. Chopped-up pieces of piping and root balls littered the room. All the light fixtures had been ripped out, their ballasts torn from their mounts. The fans and tanks had been dragged out, too, but there in the rubble strewn about the floor, he found what he was looking for. Dozens and dozens of branches and tops had fallen in the massacre. He was rich already, but it was unlike JJ to leave a job unfinished. He filled two thirty-three-gallon bags to the brim, taking every little smashed and stepped-on bud he could find, grabbed a bag of personal belongings and a flat of rooted cuttings, then returned to the ground-floor exit and ran like the wind for the woods. Once inside the tree line, he stopped and watched for a while before taking his booty to the stashed company van. He sat in the driver's seat and fully intended to drive away, but that unattended garden, just sitting there, was too much to resist. The second time he snuck in, he didn't even run. He dismantled two complete systems and carried them into the woods. He got away clean, but, like an addicted gambler, he had to return. Two more systems made it safely into the truck before he got carried away with himself. Then he started pulling out systems whole and dragging them, still wired, into the forest, where he piled up sixteen more and the entire home entertainment system before daylight brought another county crew to finish the job. They must have been shocked when they found it partially dismantled and missing every high-tech piece of gear that hadn't been nailed down.

# CHAPTER 16

Fingerprints and photographs are really more humiliating than you expect. They pass you around like meat going to market. Everyone you come in contact with treats you like the lowliest worm on the planet. Kassen shoved me from station to station like a prize puppy on display. It was more humbling than I had imagined, but I had done just that so many times before that I was prepared. I ignored his digs and insults and resisted the temptation to defend myself, and before long, I ended up in a large office cubicle. Its free-standing panel walls fell short of the ceiling and were clear plastic from half-way up, allowing the whole force to file by and alternately sneer and chuckle at me. Soon enough, Kassen and Nolan came in with an older local sheriff's deputy. They hit me with two hours of questions about the project and about Chet, Jim, and Patrick, as well as about myself. Just to get me riled up, they said they knew I was a coke dealer. And they told me that Patrick had ratted me out, which I already knew to be true. But mostly, they wanted to know where Chet sold the weed and where all the money was.

I didn't say a word to those fuckers and couldn't have answered those questions if I'd wanted to. It was a textbook example of how to clam up, brought on by years of watching other idiots do otherwise. Most recently, Patrick's bout of oral diarrhea. When Kassen finally erupted with frustration from me saying, "I have nothing to say," I turned to the deputy, and, conceding that I might be in some trouble, I requested a lawyer's presence and refused to utter another word. They paraded Patrick by the window and into another room, this one behind a real wall but with an adjacent window so we could see each other. He screamed, "I didn't tell them nothing, man," but I just burned him with a death ray.

All the lawyer info had been worked out in advance, but I never got a chance to call. They took the only home address and phone number I could give them, my father's, kept me in a cell for the rest of the weekend, and turned me loose with no charges on Monday morning, at 10 a.m., admonishing me to stay in town. I fIgured they wanted to see if I would panic and do something stupid or incriminating like leading them to the money or trying to contact Chet, so I didn't know where to go. My residence for over two years had been that lumber mill, and I had no other home. I certainly couldn't go to Drake's, or to Charlie's in the mountains, though I wanted to get hold of her to fInd out if she was okay. The Hilton with my fortune and a huge hash stash in it had been seized, and I was left with only one-hundred-and-forty bucks in my wallet.

I caught a bus back to Berkeley and called Winston for a ride. He arrived in a shiny, new, white, convertible Lexus, driven by an equally shiny, new, white girl. She was the cookie-cutter image of hundreds of other coeds who came to U.C. Berkeley from a thousand white-bread communities who just couldn't resist the idea of being fucked by a big, bad black man. And Winston was only too happy to oblige.

I planned to crash at his place for a couple of days until I figured out what was going on. I figured they'd want my ass sooner than later, but the call never came. Days turned into weeks, which in turn, became months. Winston and his tribe treated me like a king. He made a big deal about my being a hero in the struggle for herb, one step ahead of the law for years, now caught in the clutches of the system. They lavished me with praise and attention and love and anything else they could. They expressed their solidarity and sorrow, but no one could have been sorrier for me than me.

As time went on, the pressure build-up was enormous. Those fuckin' cops were good at what they did, and they did it with glee. First, they had convinced themselves that pot was terrible and growers were evil, then, having demonized us, any behavior on their part became justified. They knew that while the time passes easily for them, it was a torturous rack for their victims. While you waited to do your time, you were wrecked financially, your marriage fell apart, your friends deserted you—or worse, turned on you—and your employer fired you. But it's worse on the kids. They had no qualms about wrecking your life, and they couldn't care less about the hardships they put on the innocent children. For growing a harmless herb! It was absurd! But it was real. Potheads were going to jail by the hundreds of thousands. I had one of the best lawyers around, one who had no tolerance for finks and wouldn't just plead the client out, but with no charges, there was nothing for her to do. I wanted her to pursue the U.S. Assistant District Attorney about the case, but she advised me to let sleeping dogs lie, and five months of me burning up her telephone line with useless questions was hard on everyone. I relied on her for support because the rest of my network had broken down. Winston had only heard from JJ one time. He said he was going underground until he was sure it was safe to come up. He had good wishes for me, but it was useless to risk his freedom hanging about. That was perfectly reasonable to me. In fact, picturing Jimmy "underground" on some Mexican beach with his tall glass of Dos Equis in one hand, in the shade of one of those little drink umbrellas, and a young, long-legged Latina in the other brought a smile to my otherwise dour mug. Face it. I wasn't very good at handling these troubles. I was moody and depressed. I ate hardly anything, and sleeping was iffy, at best. Ideally, I could have been stronger, but that just wasn't my nature. My emotions got the best of me, and I couldn't hide it. Charlie had made contact, but she was also very nervous and returned to the mountains for the duration. As for Chet, not a word. My lawyer's fee was paid by wire transfer the day I got out, and then, as if he were in cahoots with the cops, silence. Repressive silence for nearly five, long months.

There was always a crowd at Winston's place, a condemnable block of four storefronts that he had turned into rehearsal studios for local bands. Seven or more people lived there at any one time, and a wider circle of close friends used the maze of rooms as a clubhouse. A large, upstairs office with exposed beams and the roof for a ceiling served as Winston's lair. What had once been a rundown, old, warehouse loft was reborn into a ragamuffin paradise. Using cheap tapestries and billowing scarves, posters, soft light, and throw-away furniture, he had created a funky, cozy, warm space that you really wanted to hang out in. He had to climb up a three-and-a-half-foot wall and go through a curtain of beads on his knees to enter the boxed-out skylight, just the size of an eastern king mattress that served as his bed. It was draped with yards of colorful scrap fabric. Pillows huge and small lined the walls with lots of baubles, dangling jewelry, and glass prisms to catch the light. Girls couldn't resist it. They were magnetically drawn to it like a moth to sunlight. Once caught in the web, they found it difficult to escape. He wasn't pushy. They just offered themselves like gifts, and he was casual in his acceptance. Mine was a room off of his parlor, so I was able to see the parade first-hand. They came in all sizes, shapes, colors, and nationalities. From a Swedish exchange student to a Chinese-American post-graduate to the occasional hot sister from the hood. Cum one, cum all! Watching all those fine women file through and overhearing the occasional romp just added to the intense pressure. I probably should have jumped right in, but I wouldn't let down enough to enjoy myself.

It was always very noisy in the complex, and I had gotten used to the din, so I figured the ruckus that woke me early one morning was more serious than usual. A bunch of Winston's friends were shouting angrily, and things were crashing around. I made my way downstairs and found four of them circled around one poor fellow who was on his knees and elbows, protecting his head with his hands, while they gave him a pretty good beating.

"Please," he cried. "I'm just a messenger!"

One of Winston's friends kicked him again and shouted, "Then why you sneakin' 'round here like a fuckin' thief?"

"I'm looking for Jason Garrett!" he pleaded. "I don't mean no harm." They stopped pummeling him for a minute. He was dressed in completely different clothes—a cheap, wrinkled suit replaced the tie-dye, and with no beanie to cover the balding head, he looked older and straighter than at our last meeting. Now, on his knees with blood dripping from a gash over his right eye, he was somehow less menacing. "My name is Mountain," he said. "Tell 'im! Tell 'im Mountain has a message for 'im!" He looked up, saw me standing halfway up the stairs, and reached out his hand to me.

My protectors all looked at me for confirmation. "Never seen him before," I said, and boots rained down on him again. "Hold it! Hold it!" I jumped down and pulled them off him. "I know this fool."

"Oh, man. Why didn't you say so?" they asked.

I lifted his head by the hair and looked straight into his face, "because I don't like the way he delivers messages." I led Mountain up to my room, and two of the girls in the crew tended to his cut. He wasn't as full of piss and vinegar as before. In fact, he was quite contrite in the delivery of his message. It seemed Chet was finally ready to make contact. I yelled at Mountain, cursing Chet at the top of my lungs. "Now he wants to see me!? Now that I've been left in the desert to die of thirst! You tell that son of a bitch he made me some promises he damned well better keep!" Mountain tried to interrupt, but I snapped at him, and he held his tongue. "I trusted his word and grew a fortune for him, and if he doesn't come through for me now, there will be hell to pay."

Mountain recognized empty threats when he heard them, so he didn't react to my anger. "He's been watching," Mountain said. "He's sending me for you now." He handed me the message this time. It was long and full of cryptic instructions.

I crumpled it up and tossed it back at him. "You tell Chet that if he wants me to do his bidding for him, he'd better come tell me in person."

"No, he won't come out into the open. You know that," he replied.

"I expect him to fulfill his promise to me," I said. "I have lost everything, and my ass is in a sling. This is no time to fuck around. If he has a plan, let's hear it." Mountain had nothing to say to assuage my anger, so he kept quiet. In my disgust, I gave up on him and Chet. "Get out!" I said, throwing his jacket in his lap. "Get out now! And tell my old friend I said thanks anyway. He's done enough damage to my life. Tell him to enjoy the millions I made him and just leave me holding the bag." He tried to speak again, but I shouted him down, "Get out!" I could feel my face turn red with anger. "Now!" Having not accomplished his mission, this trained spook tried to explain, but my housemates heard me yelling and appeared behind him. "Show this gentleman to the door," I said. Mountain took one look at his attackers and gave up.

"I'll tell 'im," he said.

"You do that," I said. As he turned for the door, I flashed back to the Jerry Show and the knife in my ribs. I kicked him hard in the ass as he left. "And give him one of these for me."

* * * * * * *

It was a much-needed relief to tell Chet to fuck off, even if it was by proxy. But that night when the rush wore off, I found myself alone in my room and, being adopted by Winston's family notwithstanding, I felt more alone than I ever had. My lawyer was the only one left fighting for me, and she was a hired hand. I lay awake most of the night and couldn't even get out of bed the next morning. My new crew got me up around midday and spent quite a bit of time with me arguing the merits of skipping the country. Their points were solid. One, I hadn't been charged in six months, so I could hardly be hit with evading prosecution. Two, it was only a seven-year wait for the statute of limitations to run out. And three, Amsterdam ain't such a bad place! I was paralyzed into inaction. Awash in doubt and fear. Alone and not confident in my own judgment.

But that all changed that same afternoon when a loud knock came at the front door of the studio. Several of my buddies answered, while I listened from above. The oddly dressed citizen of slight build looked unthreatening enough through the peephole, but they recognized the nervous-looking dude with the bandage on his head as the guy they had roughed up earlier. The doorman hollered for help, and by the time the door opened, Chester Hawthorne found himself confronted by half a dozen angry men ready to fight. Winston looked right past Chet at Mountain. "You haven't had enough?" he said.

Mountain started to answer from behind Chet's shoulder, but Chet raised a gloved hand to silence him. Mountain took that as a signal to beat a hasty retreat and returned to the black Lincoln Town Car parked at the curb. My protectors grew anxious and demanded that Chet state his business, but he was blind to their impatience and waited until Mountain was safely away before he spoke.

"I am a friend of Jason's, and I'm here to speak with him," he said with patient arrogance.

Several of the guys came through the doorway and stood shoulder to shoulder between Chet and the entrance, forming an imposing barrier. One of them shouted, "You don't fuckin' get it, do you? He said he don't have nothing to say to you!"

Chet paused for an interminable time. They half-surrounded him in a threatening manner, but he remained calm and deliberate. Looking down, leaving himself completely unprotected, he slowly removed his tight, leather gloves one finger at a time and placed them in the pocket of his dark-gray trench coat. Then he carefully reached into his breast pocket, causing his aggressors to shift uncomfortably, and removed a silver cigarette case and a fancy lighter. Plucking a Gauloises from the case and placing it in his mouth, he lifted his head, revealing his eyes under the brim of his hat, struck the lighter, and lit the cigarette while they stood there and watched. He took a long drag as he looked into the eyes of two large gentlemen who blocked his way. Then he deliberately blew the smoke straight ahead and began to walk right between them as if the smoke would clear his path. The two men flinched, not believing his boldness, and he confidently strode by. "Tell him his pal is here," he ordered over his shoulder.

They rushed into the office behind him, angrily cussing, and they would have attacked him if I hadn't got there in time. That could've been ugly, as they took Chet lightly, a very dangerous thing to do. I introduced him to everyone as one of my best friends and smoothed over all the tension, thanking them for looking after my welfare.

When I got him into the upstairs parlor, Chet never even mentioned the unfriendly welcome or Mountain's bloody eye, preferring to get right to the point. "Getting anxious, huh?" he said with a grin.

"Yes. I'm anxious!" I half-yelled. "I'm out here all alone!"

"I got you a lawyer didn't I?" He remained calm.

"A lotta' fuckin' good that's doin'!" I said, my temper rising.

"Calm down, pal," he cooed. "I'm right here. I haven't forgotten you."

"You son of a bitch," I screamed. "You promised me. You guaranteed I wouldn't get busted!"

"No. I never said that," he countered.

I couldn't believe what I was hearing from this man I loved and trusted as a mentor, but my anger melted to sorrow, and I began to fall apart. "You promised!" I said through tears. "And now I'm fucked!" Sorrow turned to resignation.

He moved beside me, and, putting his arm around me, he bade me to buck up. "I know I did, Jase. I promised you would be okay. Don't worry. I can fix this. It's going to be okay. But I never said you wouldn't get busted."

He was still making promises, and though I still wanted to believe him, it was downright impossible. "How?!" I cried out. "How can you fix this?"

"It's all part of the program," he said. "Everything will be all right, but I'll need your help. You have to pull yourself together, and we can beat this thing."

I was starting to feel better. Maybe it wasn't all so bleak. Maybe Chet would surprise me and figure a way out. I wiped away the tears and straightened myself up. "What do you want me to do?"

"I have a mission for you," he said, and it was clear he did have a plan.

# CHAPTER 17

There it was. Right where Chet said it would be. A small placard, hewn by hand, on a piece of scrap plywood nailed twenty feet high in the Ironwoods that protect the wharf at Kealakekua Bay. I was to begin my mission by talking to whoever was sitting at the wooden table and benches under this sign marked "HHH." The letters meant nothing to me, save they lay on my road to salvation, but now as I approached a man seated on the table, the rest of the words came into view, "Hawaiian Head Hunters."

"You want sometin, bra?" the man said, snapping me back to the present. I was a little flustered, as my mind hadn't quite digested the idea of cannibalism. He was a small guy for a Hawaiian. Probably about forty, but weathered. He was three cans into a six-pack of Budweiser and smoking a Kool from a pack of cigarettes tucked into the chest pocket of his Hawaiian shirt, which lay on the table. A pair of mid-length shorts, worn beach walkers, and a touristy, sun-visor hat reading "Kona" completed the ensemble.

CHAPTER 17 

"Yeah. Ah, how you doin', my friend?" I tried to sound as friendly as possible. "My name is Jason Garrett."

"Another beautiful day in paradise," he said with a trace of sarcasm in his voice.

"I'm, ah, looking for someone," I stammered.

"There ain't nobody 'round here," he said without even looking. There was no aloha here, but I had been through plenty already, and with miles to go, this joker wasn't going to stop me now.

"No, I'm looking for someone in particular, and I was told the Hawaiian Head Hunters would be able to help me locate him. You know these Hawaiian Head Hunters?"

"Da' HHH ain't no lost-and-found, bra'." He acted insulted, but it was just bravado.

\* \* \* \* \* \* \*

Chet had sent me on a quest, the holy grail of which was a man he called Picnic. A highly trained intelligence operative whose talents in the field of deception were so valuable that they became dangerous to have. A man who, he assured me, held the key to unlock the cell that awaited me. He gave me no description, no picture, no address, no phone number. Just the name, the initials HHH, this location, and a gold medallion that he said would identify me, which he pressed carefully into my palm. It was a five-pointed star surrounded by a green laurel wreath. Inside the star, a woman's head was circled by the words, "United States Of America." Before the sun had set on me twice, I found myself soaring over the black volcanic desert of the Kohala coast on approach to Keahole International Airport on the dry side of the Big Island of Hawaii.

The instant they opened the aircraft's doors, the island's humidity informed me that my mainland clothes would serve me poorly in the tropics. With only one carry-on, I skipped the baggage drama but had to wait until I picked up my tiny, economy-class rental clunker to change into shorts and sandals. Pretending the low-grade stash that Winston turned me on to was the spicy, rich, Hawaiian herb I hoped was in my near future, I cruised down the highway, almost forgetting there was another shoe due to drop.

This Picnic guy, a former member of the American intelligence community, was such a hot property that he had to hide from his own agency, which would have liked nothing better than to overuse him until he burned out and then discard him. Chet said he was a human chameleon, whatever that meant, "an ability more like a sickness that the victim can't control." When I queried further, he said it was like having the power to be invisible, and he refused to comment more. This really intrigued me. A literal interpretation seemed absurd, but what other interpretation was there? Picnic had chosen this hundred-mile strip of outlaw territory as his refuge and the Head Hunters, I now assumed, as his protectors. Somehow he was supposed to set me free, but getting to him was proving a mite tricky.

\* \* \* \* \* \* \*

I figured this Hawaiian guy had pegged me for a hick and so determined that it would take something of a different approach to get through to him. Without really thinking it out, I climbed up onto the table and sat beside him, looking out over his ocean domain. Without asking, I pulled a beer from its plastic loop and popped the tab. This took him by surprise, but before he could protest, I took a big swig and said, "Ahh... beautiful view, huh?"

He got all ruffled, but he still called me "bra'." "What da' hell you t'ink you doin', bra'? You don' know me!"

I gave him the coolest smile ever and said slowly, with perfect timing such as I had never achieved before, "I'm gonna sit right here and drink all your beer until you decide to hook me up with the HHH, if only to save yourself from dying of thirst." I figured, what the hell, even if he punched me in the head, it would be worth it to get on to where I was going.

In the silence that ensued, he stared me down so I would've sworn he was going to eat me, but, as it turned out, he decided he liked me. He got up and began to laugh in a very melodramatic way, stammering around and talking out loud to me and some imaginary friend who was sharing the joke, "Ah, hah-hah, you see this boule? He ton ta don! You got balls, eh *haole*? I like dat'. You all right, bra'," he said and clinked his beer against mine roughly enough to spill it. "I'm gonna help you, 'my friend'," he mocked in his best *haole* voice, "yes, I am. But you gotta come back here tomorrow 'round dis' time."

"What then?" I didn't like being left in the dark.

"Then what, you see. Jus' be here, bra'." Sensing he was finished with me, I turned to go, but he stopped me, "Hey, bra'! Bring da' beer."

"Sure ting, bra." I could mock, as well. I drank my beer and tossed the empty into a nearby, chicken-wire garbage can that was filled with aluminum containers. "Don't worry, my friend. I'll be here." As I drove away, I couldn't help but wonder if he'd be waiting with three big mokes to kick my ass when I returned. Some people can be pretty particular about who they share their beer with, and I had acted with the manners of a wild boar. Soon after I drove away I found a choppy, little side-road that headed in the direction of the beach, and though it was a rough, volcanic rock track and densely overgrown on both sides, I turned the ill-equipped mini-car in hopes of finding a place to hole up. The road was seldom used, as branches flogged either side of the vehicle like a car wash, reaching through the window a few times to smack me in the face. Before long, the road turned south along the coastline and broke into the clear. I had to maneuver the fragile vehicle carefully on the intensely uneven, hard, rock road, which traveled along the top of a twenty-foot cliff about fifty feet from the edge. Almost immediately, I came to a spot on the cliff top where the lava had naturally created a three-foot, indented area that resembled a sunken living room. Sand cast ashore by waves crashing against the island had collected over time and created a tent-size beach atop the cliff, and although I had no tent, I stashed the car in the jungle by the side of the road and, after a mini-mart meal, crashed in the sand for the night, needing only my clothes to keep warm.

I had no idea where I was or what was coming next. In fact, my whole life was in doubt. But this night of sleep was not fitful like so many that had come since the flak-jacketed, black-booted thugs had invaded my dreams. The ocean roared to my side, and the island trembled below, but I slept like a big dog on a hot day until I awoke with the birds at first light. Local kids were playing in the water nearby and having no problem with me camping there. In fact, they took great pride in showing me the best places to launch myself off the cliff, which they called the "pali," and leading me into underwater lava tubes that penetrated the island wall.

The day passed slowly. The heat could bake you even in the shade. My young friends brought me a lunch of strawberry papaya and young coconut they called "spoon meat" that had the consistency of Jell-O, but tasted like coconut, sugar and butter. When they saw that I had salsa and tortilla chips, they split for a minute, only to return with an avocado nearly the size of my head. They split it in half, pitted it, and filled it with salsa. We attacked it with our tortilla knives until it was gone, and then I shared the remainder of the chocolates and caramel corn I had bought for the plane, which they gobbled up with great enthusiasm.

Soon enough, the time came for me to face whatever was next. I dragged my compact out of the bushes and stopping only for the beer, made my way back to the table that served as HHH headquarters. Only tourists were milling around the wharf when I arrived. I parked myself at the table like a local and waited. Carloads of tourists invaded the tiny village one after another. Brightly bathing-suited vacationers leapt out of shining, red convertibles and sparkling, white mini-vans with rented water gear of all varieties, only to find out there was no picturesque, white-sand beach for towel laying, or for that matter, any convenient entry point. Hence, after much milling about and pebble kicking, they piled back into their Trojan horses and headed off to the next spot on the tourist trail, nicely plotted for them on brightly colored maps provided at the hotels, condos, and car shops.

My "bra'"—his name was Freddie—pulled in about an hour late in an older, brown, four-wheel pick-up, pock-marked from years of hard driving but still running like a champ and—by the sound of her —more powerful than was necessary. He slid to a stop in the gravel, raising a small dust cloud that drifted over the gawking haoles lingering at the wharf.

"Hey, bra'," he called through the open passenger window, as he turned down the strange mixture of Hawaiian and reggae music that was blaring from the tape deck. "You like come with me?" It wasn't really a question. Tossing my bag in the back and climbing in, I left my wheels behind, and so my own agenda. I was on Freddie's time now. We were going where he wanted, on his time schedule. I was completely at his mercy and not too comfortable about it. He headed south on the main highway for about half-an-hour to a poorly marked turn-off that led to a very small village of about twenty houses that were on the water. They were separated from the luxuries of county water and electricity by the half-mile-wide lava flow into which they were carved. The road was paved over the hills and trenches created by the once-surging lava, making it feel like the truck was surfing over rock waves as we passed. The people who lived there knew Freddie and his truck well, but they stared at me like a zoo animal, making it clear that tourists were not exactly welcome there. A community pavilion was at road's end, where small fishing boats lay along the water's edge and nets hung, awaiting repair. He pointed to a trail that continued where the road stopped and then said, "We walk," so I strapped my duffel bag over my shoulder, and we began. The trail crossed over two small, sandy coves before climbing up onto an older flow that had completely grown over with large-thorned Kiawe trees laced with vines of passion fruit and then down the other side into fairly dense jungle. The trail, my guide informed me, was once part of the king's trail that was laid in ancient times and circled the island. "Anyone who failed to prostrate themselves before these 'Alii' as they passed," he continued, "would lose their heads." I wondered if this could be my fate. I asked if the elusive Mr. Picnic was down this trail, but he only said this was "the way." A quarter-mile in, we climbed onto a third flow. This one must have been a mere couple hundred years old, as it was still shiny black and empty as night. The hot sun beat down from above and radiated with equal intensity from below. Sweat poured off my face, and I was glad to get back into the trees after only a few hundred feet of exposure. Finally, we passed some giant knots of night-blooming cactus, with their long arms weaving across the lava and through the trees, before we arrived at a beautiful crescent beach of dark sand. It was sprinkled with coconut palms and alive with dozens of people, big and small, involved in daily activities. I noticed the enticing scent of a barbeque burning. Small huts thatched with palm fronds dotted the back line of the beach where the sand gave way to the jungle, and most of the toin' and froin' was aimed at them. Though everyone noticed me, unlike the village behind, they didn't seem to care. That was fine with me. I was more concerned with getting a look at what was on that grill, which remained just out of view. We crossed to the other end of the beach and climbed a lava embankment that formed the bay's southernmost peninsula. There we came to a shack for which, I'm sure, the word ramshackle was invented. It was only slightly larger than a two-car garage and constructed completely of used wood that looked as though it had drifted up onto this remote shore and been installed one piece at a time. As we walked around it, I found the structure lay at the edge of a vast flow, where the jungle gave way to the fury of once-molten rock. From this vantage, I could see that this flow and the one we had crossed on foot were one and the same. The volcano had buried a swath of land two miles wide near the sea, sparing just this oasis, which only stretched from here to the truck parked back at the pavilion.

We entered the shack through what served as a door, yet it had no latch or strike. A hooked nail served as doorknob, making it more of a gate. A lantern hanging on a wall nail was the only visible means of generated light, needless during the day, as the walls were downright porous and let in plenty of light. The interior had been crudely divided into two rooms. In the doorway between them hung a curtain made of a flowered sheet or possibly an old sarong, which Freddie pulled aside, ushering me in to the room nearest the beach. A mattress lay in one corner, and piles of clothes and gear lined the walls, leaving two, old, straight-back wooden chairs as the only furniture. My benefactor told me to wait and left me to sit alone for nearly half an hour. The smell of something exquisite sizzling on that fire wafted through the walls, drawing my attention to an off-triangular hole in the wall that served as a window. The fire pit was situated on the flat, dry part of the beach under the palms, a few feet from where it began to slope down to the water. My view of it was obstructed, but oh, what an obstruction. A beautiful, young, Hawaiian woman with long, thick, black hair and a narrow frame captured my attention. She wore an ankle-length print wrap knotted at the hip and a plain, brown bikini top that tied around the back of the neck and revealed a flat belly and slender back the color of the perfect tan. I began to salivate as I studied her graceful movements and joyous demeanor with the group assembled for the evening meal, and I wasn't sure if I was hungrier or hornier, but before I had a chance to fantasize about either, my host returned.

"And he's a little bit of a wise ass," I heard Freddie say, just as the sheet parted and his grinning face appeared. The floor of the shack, which was built stronger than it looked and only squeaked softly when I had entered, complained loudly now, and the building shifted noticeably toward the front door as his companion came into the shack. An instant hallucination of me floating in a bubbling cauldron with a stalk of celery and a bunch of carrots flashed through my consciousness as my host entered the doorway. He was the biggest man I had ever seen. At six-two and well over four hundred pounds, he filled the entrance and was unable to walk through square-shouldered. I unconsciously backed away with my mouth agape and hadn't caught my breath before a second giant appeared. This man was visibly larger than the one before, by weight and height, and had a difficult time negotiating the frame at all, the top of which came only to his shoulder, and with a width that barely allowed for sidestepping. One of them had on baggy, cotton, mid-length shorts, the other a huge bolt of blue-jean overalls, and both wore tee-shirts of the multi-X variety. Neither had shoes, as no shoe I had ever seen would have fit them, and around their necks both wore Hawaiian fishhooks hand-carved from fish bone. The first guy, the brains of the bunch—it only took two to make a bunch—took a position in front of me and had a jovial demeanor for such an imposing figure. The larger man, who turned out to be the younger of the two brothers, took up a more intimidating angle behind me. He was just out of view over my right shoulder and close enough that I could hear his strained breathing.

"Ass' da' guy?" the older brother asked. Freddie sat backwards on one of the chairs, resting his arms and head on the backrest.

"Ass' 'im," he answered.

"You looking for the HHH," the big guy said.

These guys looked more like the Huge Hulking Hawaiians, but I resisted the nervous urge to joke. "Hi. I'm Jason Garrett. I was hoping you would lead me to a friend of mine, name of Picnic." I was somehow less demanding now.

"Dis' man you seek, how you know 'im?" he asked.

"I don't actually know him," I answered sheepishly. They looked at Freddie, confused, so I tried to explain. "He is a friend of my good friend, and I'm supposed to give him a message." They weren't convinced. "This man Picnic who I never met has a good friend who is in trouble and asked me to give this to him." I showed them the medallion.

He took it, giving it a good examination. "You give it ta' me an I'll see he gets it, bra'," he said with the intonation of a man whose word is law.

"No, no!" I protested, forgetting myself and grabbing it out of his hand.

Little brother snatched me off my feet from behind, held me helplessly off the floor, wriggling like a hooked fish, and grunted a warning in my ear. My questioner chuckled at my disobedience, and, putting his huge hand on my head, he messed up my hair like a little boy's. "He's tougher than he is smart," he said to Freddie, knowing I'd get the point. I stopped struggling, and little brother, who was able to maintain control of me with his hands alone, tossed me into the empty chair like a dirty pair of pants and hovered over me. I started to get up again, but an enormous but gentle hand on my shoulder anchored me to my seat.

"Jus' hold on, little bra'. Don' get excited." The sumo behind me spoke softly, almost whispering, in a pitch too high for the grand scale of his body.

"No *pilikia* (problem), bra'," the older brother said, attempting to settle me down before I did something I'd regret. I struggled a little further. "Bra!" He raised his voice. "You say you're a friend, and I'm willin' to take your word, but if you keep actin' a fool, I'll have to pound you jus' on principal. Friend or no."

I capitulated. Not that I had the slightest choice. "All right, all right!" I said. "I'm cool, I'm cool."

"That's better, little bra', easy," junior said, as though he were soothing his pet kitten, while giving my shoulder a little squeeze that felt more like a clamp.

"Now, we can get a message to dis' man you seek, but it will take some time, bra'." He tried to reassure me, as I was probably looking pretty scared.

"Some time?" I asked.

"Yeah, bra'," he said. "Maybe a day or two." I guess I looked crestfallen, so he continued, "You can stay here, bra', with us. My name is Albert, and this is my little brother, Ruben. You'll have no problems, bra'. Jus' relax. Enjoy this tropical heaven." I'm sure my expression was not that of gratitude, when it should have been. "Come with me." He sidled through the door. Ruben lifted me to my feet like a two-year-old and helped me through the door.

"Thanks," I said, straightening my collar. We walked out on the ply-scrap-covered wood pallets that served as the front porch, and Albert gave me a guided tour of the area by finger point. The cooking area, the sleeping quarters, the best place to go for a swim, etc. But my attention was fixated on the food. "You think you could treat me to a meal?" I asked.

"Ho, bra'! You gone hungry?" he asked. "Jus' go over der' and introduce yourself to our *ohana*," he said. "Tell em you like *kow kow*. We gon take care a you, little bra'." He turned my shoulder in the right direction and gave me a helpful push, like you would a toy truck. "Go on now, bra'. No *pilikia*."

They turned out to be nice enough guys, but their virtual hugeness made it hard to believe. I made my way over to the grill and was almost moved to tears by the sight of it. A variety of colorful reef fish laid whole over the fire, not one of them greater than a half-pound. The grillsman only added salt, then let them burn. To the side of the fire sat a pot of rice large enough to feed a parade and a smaller pot bubbling with a dark amber-colored sauce. I circled the fire pit like a starving shark, not knowing exactly where to attack. Twenty or so adults were concentrating on their plates while an equal complement of kids skirmished around the edges of the beach. None of them paid me any attention as I approached the stack of paper plates and waited shyly for the chef to notice me, looking like a begging dog.

"Here, let me help." A voice came from behind, as a hand reached around my waist and relieved me of my flatware. "You have the look of a very hungry man," she said. I turned to face her as she came up beside me, and our eyes met for a second before she looked away. "We'll fix that," she said, as she slapped a whole, sizzling, little, black-and-orange fish on the plate, the head and tail still on it, followed by a large serving of rice. On top of this she drizzled the sauce. Then she took something off the coals that looked like a basketball wrapped in tin foil. When she carefully lifted the top off it, the way you would the lid from a jack-o-lantern, it released a smell that took me back to my mother's pumpkin pie the instant it reached my nose.

"Wow! What is that?" I asked, as she stuck in a long wooden spoon, and began to stir.

"Hawaiian squash," she said, looking up with a smile. "I know you're going to love it." She withdrew the spoon and held it up to my lips, cupping her free hand under my chin should any spill. "Here, taste," she offered. It didn't matter how hungry I was at that point. Even with the strong smell of cinnamon drifting up my nose, it was her I wanted a taste of. As she coaxed my mouth open with the spoon, I stared straight into her eyes.

"There you go," she cooed, studying my face for a reaction. "How's that?"

"Mam...Just like mom's punkin' pie," I answered like a happy kid.

She laughed a little but stayed right in front of me. Face to face, only a foot apart. "Is it really good?" She wanted to hear me say it again, but she had to suffer a moment for her answer while I hesitated. Taking the spoon from her hand, I dipped it again, and, putting it to my lips, I looked up, searching the ether for the perfect response. "Inspirational" was my one-word pronouncement, which she really liked, causing a really big smile and revealing for the first time the full ripeness of her lips. It was all I could do to keep myself from leaning toward her slightly, making that subtle move that would let her know I wanted to kiss her. While giving no indication that she wanted to be kissed, she didn't look away, either, but I caught myself and chickened out. I hadn't known her for five minutes, yet it was hard to contain my desire. As she heaped a full serving of squash onto my plate she said her name was Alana and that her big brothers had asked her to look after me. Then she introduced me to the people we met as we walked to a palm tree that perched over the crest of the beach providing shade as it leaned toward the sea. We were able to sit on the flat part of the sand and let our legs trail downhill, making a very comfortable spot for us to share our meal.

I tried not to gobble my food, but I was so hungry I felt weak. The food was really special, I couldn't help myself. The fish was the sweetest, juiciest white meat you can imagine and well worth the inconvenience of sifting through it for the numerous tiny bones one couldn't help but encounter. This was eaten with a large spoon of rice and mayonnaise, and it tasted out of this world by itself, but with that sauce it was fantastic. The sauce, I learned, was a homemade chutney of passion fruit and mango, spiked with little red Hawaiian peppers that was at once sweet and hot and was addictively delicious on everything. But it was no less than magnificent on the barbequed lobster that Albert laid on me as seconds.

"Spiny lobster," he said. "Bugga' don' need no butta'." And he was right. After I ripped it from its singed shell, I wasted no time digging in. I watched Big Albert devour first one, then another, holding the hapless creature like a drumstick, but I was so strung out on the chutney I had to dip.

"Oh, my God!" I dripped. "This is the most delicious thing I have ever tasted." Several of my hosts were now eating near us, and they all got a chuckle out of me.

"Broke-da-mout," Albert said.

I was embarrassed, but I didn't understand the slang, so I had to ask, "What?"

"Warp-da-jaw," he said, while I looked on quizzically.

"They all laughed again before Alana said it slowly enough for me to understand, then spelled it out, "It means it tastes good," and I felt let off the hook. We all talked and had the best laugh I'd had since the bust, aided by my first taste of the local herb provided by Ruben, who turned out to be the biggest pothead of the clan. He had some small, green budlets that unscrewed the top of my head and allowed my brain to float in moon gravity. I began to think a two-day setback might not be so bad. At least it would give Alana and me a chance to get acquainted, which we did. Like old friends long separated. With her, it was effortless to get past uneasy formality down to what was real. I always wanted to go there with people, though it seemed like a chance to take. But with Alana, it was the natural state of conversation. It would never have occurred to her to be sarcastic or cynical, and I became aware of the slightest pretense on my part. Even flirtation seemed lame and dishonest. We spent most of that time together swimming, walking the trail down the coast, exploring a dry lava tube, and each other's deepest thoughts, and the whole time I never touched her. Partly for fear her big brothers might clobber me with the wooden post they used to club any big fish they caught, but mostly because she was the sweetest, realest woman I'd ever met. The most open and most willing to be hurt, rather than be something she was not.

This became a difficult task, as two days turned into three and three into five. I became obsessed with the desire to see her face in the throes of orgasm, so much so that I began to get shaky each time our eyes met. By the sixth day, I knew if I didn't get out of there sooner, I'd have to kidnap her later and take her away with me. I confronted Albert about being stalled and feeling like a prisoner, and I probably got a little too angry, because he acted like a hurt host. He answered the way he would talk to a direction-seeking tourist, disappointed that I might be just another ugly American. "Your car is parked at the pavilion," he said. "You can go anytime you like. You like wait for your friend Picnic, it will take more time, but you still welcome here. Our *hale* (house), yo *hale*." Then he turned and walked away. Immediately I knew I had been ungracious, and I wanted to run after him to apologize, but the words would have sounded hollow, and only a long resumé of future good deeds could repair the damage. I spent another two days there, more on my own, afraid to be with Alana and then disrespect her by leaving, waiting for a second chance to prove myself worthy of the Head Hunters' aloha. Alana was a little angry, but I was able to mend some fences with her before the time came to go. We spent the night before I left together, holding hands on the still-warm beach, watching the sunset, and sharing the stars. I never did kiss her, though I knew she wanted me to.

# CHAPTER 18

I feared for my life when I saw the rusted-out bucket of bolts that came to pick me up at the pavilion, but I had already said my good-byes and thank-yous in camp as sincerely as I could muster, and walked the trail back to civilization. There was no turning back now. My car, as advertised, was right there, but Albert insisted I go in that beat-up jalopy held together with duct tape and fishing string. I had my bag packed, but Freddie said I would only be taking my best hiking shoes, long pants, a flashlight, and as many tee-shirts as I had. I would be going on a very long hike up the mountain to where Picnic lived in an encampment of Rastas, who were growing an enormous crop of herb in a place they called "Jah Valley." It seemed odd that they would take me to such a place, which would explain the long delay, but that was where Picnic was, and if I wanted to see him, I'd have to start walking.

I climbed into the back of the faded-yellow VW Rabbit, careful not to put my foot through the hole in the floorboard. It took a moment to situate myself, as it was necessary to arrange colorful carpet samples over the exposed springs sticking out of what used to be the back seat. I carried only my knapsack with the prescribed items, two bottles of water I had scrounged out of my car, and a bag of dried banana, mango, and white pineapple that Alana had given me. By this time, I had caught on that it was going to be a serious hike, and I thought myself well prepared, but when Freddie, my guide, got into the front seat, he was still wearing his normal uniform—baggy swim shorts, a plain Hawaiian shirt, and flip flops—confusing the issue.

He introduced our driver—a large, jovial, Hawaiian—as Walter, who turned to salute me with a "Shaka"—the Hawaiian hand signal for "Hang Loose"—but was unable to rotate in the Rabbit's seat. "Howsit, bra'?" he said with a welcoming laugh. "T'row da' bag anywhere." They talked directions, and when Freddie told Walter where we were to be dropped off, Walter said, "Oh, I seeee. You gon' climb da' volcano, bra'!" His wide, rotten-toothed grin enveloped the rearview mirror when he figured out my mission. I responded only with a smile. "How far you go?" he asked, and when Freddie clued him in, he continued, "No, bra'! Not many *haole* go way up der'. In fact, not many local kind make dat walk."

"Really?" was my dumbfounded reply. A stew of excitement and fear was brewing in my belly.

"Shit naw! Only way I get der' is by truck," he said.

"More up, bra,'" Freddie said. "Past da' road, tru' da 'ranch."

"Ho, you one crazy *haole*!" Walter howled, shrugging his shoulders and pulling away from the pavilion.

Every pothole we hit on the well-worn road leading back to the highway made the beat-up Rabbit knock and shake as if it would disintegrate at any moment. The fact that the shocks were nonexistent may have had something to do with that. My window was permanently affixed in the open position, which was a good thing, as it was still ninety degrees out, even though the sun was beginning to set. For nearly an hour, I watched the colorscape from the back seat lighting up the enormous Hawaiian sky and then slowly fading to darkness as we drove south toward the drop-off point. They laughed and talked most of the way, having a great time, but I couldn't understand most of it, and, at any rate, I was too nervous to laugh.

When we got close to our destination, Freddie told me to grab my bag and be ready to jump out. He ignored my nagging questions about where we were and what the plan was and would say only that we were about to bail out of Walter's limo up ahead. Walter quickly pulled off into the gravel on the side of the highway, scraping branches against the side of the car. I followed Freddie's lead and, with a hasty *mahalo* to Walter, we bounced out of the car and crouched in the roadside bushes. Walter was gone before any traffic caught up with us, and it seemed that our attempt to be clandestine was a success. We waited in the for a few cars to pass. While he surveyed the area, I let my eyes adjust to the darkness.

"It's over der'," Freddie said after a moment.

"What?" I asked.

"Dat's where we go over," he answered, pointing to a locked, chain-link gate that was the only break in the six-foot-high fence that lined the uphill, or mauka, side of the highway, dividing it from the jungle.

"Over?" I said.

"Yeah. Right over da' gate, but der' are a few houses on da' other side, so you have to be kinda' quiet and run for da' bushes as soon as you get over."

Before I could argue, a lone car cruised by, and as soon as it passed, Freddie took off like a rabbit. A surge of adrenaline picked me up and carried me across the highway. As I ran, I saw him scurry over the top like a twenty-year-old and thought it looked easy, so without even pausing, I tossed the knapsack over and, with a leap, hit the top bar with enough force to flip over it like an Olympic gymnast on the high bar. And I could have pulled off the illusion of complete control had the recoiling gate not caught my shirt, tearing it to shreds on the way down and turning the landing, which I had planned to "stick," into a one-point landing that almost broke my butt bone. Freddie had already scurried into the brush by the time I hit the ground. He was out of sight, but I could hear him snickering. I fetched my bag and hurried to catch up so we could make a run for it, but he was laughing too hard to travel. I looked around to see if anyone had heard me. There were a few small lights that must have been houses twinkling through the jungle just up the road, but there was no movement. I scanned back to the gate. Freddie was mumbling through laughter about how funny I looked going over that fence, and I couldn't understand, but laughter is contagious, so when the fear subsided, I began to laugh right along with him.

It was only a minute or so before Freddie began to scamper up the dirt road. We passed quietly by some houses on the left and a barking dog somewhere on the right, but in a few minutes, we passed all signs of civilization, with deep jungle on both sides. After a while Freddie said it was OK to talk, but we kept it to a whisper. It was necessary to switch on our lights, as the road was rocky and difficult. He kept a hot pace. I lost my breath in the first ten minutes, as I followed his near-naked feet back and forth across the hump in the middle of the road. I caught a second wind and was right behind him after he paused for a moment, about half-an-hour in. I had already worked up a sweat and was feeling pretty good. I asked all my normal questions. Where were we? Where were we going? How far was it? But all he would say was, "More high, bra'," so I resigned myself not to ask again. Instead, I took a moment to look around. The beam of my light disappeared into blackness when I shone it back toward the highway. A barbed-wire fence separated us from the jungle on either side, which was twenty feet high, making the road feel like a dark tunnel. The air hung heavy with moisture but was really stagnant from the lack of wind. The temperature had cooled some after sundown, but it was still comfortable hiking weather, and now, with the paranoia receding, I was ready to go when Freddie began the upward trek again.

I felt like Superman for the next half-hour, filling my lungs and riding high on the long-atrophied muscles that seemed to attend indoor gardening, until the road began to climb and became more overgrown. Rocks the size of softballs lay loose in the way, creating more of a hazard and making the going that much more difficult and after stumbling on a few of them, my right knee started to hurt. When I asked how much further, Freddie said we were almost to the top, so I muzzled my complaints and stayed in step until the road came over a rise and leveled out about an hour-and-a-half in. The moment we crested the hill, I smelled pot. Not the sweet, sticky smell of pot growing, but the thick, swirling, chocolate smell of burning pot.

Freddie sat in the middle of the road, breathing hard and saying with relief, "I ain't never gonna do dat' again, bra'." I hung back on the edge of his fl ashlight glow, remaining silent while adrenaline ran laps through my system. At fi rst, I wondered if Freddie was talking to his imaginary "bra" again. Then I noticed the familiar flare of a burning cherry brighten the shadows just feet from Freddie's side and realized we weren't alone. A pair of large, white eyes appeared in the cherry-glow, and the dark outline of a face began to speak.

"I tell you, mon," His voice was low and warm.

"Dis' *kanaka* boy stay more *makai* (ocean) side from now on," Freddie swore. The face began to laugh, revealing those bright teeth, "Butchu' made it, mon. Gve thanks and praises." He passed a big, fat joint the size of my thumb to Freddie, who had collapsed on his back. "Ere'," he said, "da' rejuvenation."

The stranger wasn't at all surprised when I stepped out of the shadow. The uncomfortable moment before introductions was exaggerated by Freddie's coughing—more like those convulsings of a borderline emphysemic—so I introduced myself. "Hi, I'm Jason. Chester Hawthorne sent me…" I would have launched into the whole story if he hadn't stopped me.

"Yes, mon," he said, rising to his feet and into the circle of light. He clasped my hand in both of his and continued, "I bin' waitin for you 'ere, mon. I don know who you are, but you knowin' someone if you makin dis' 'ere journey wit' me."

"Yeah, yeah, yeah. Jason, this is Dodge. He's gonna' take you ta' da' top," Freddie said with still-halting breath.

I looked at Freddie incredulously, as he took another deep draw and began to recoil again. "Here, let me help you with that," I said, relieving him of the joint. "I thought you said this was the top."

"No, no, no!" they both said, one with a "bra," the other with a "mon."

Freddie was in no shape to talk, so Dodge explained. "Dis' is da' top," he said. "Da' top of da' bottom." That warm grin returned to his face, unveiling an inner wisdom that made me trust this complete stranger. I asked how much further, and he said, "It's no problem, mon. Jus a likkle more up den' tru' da jungle a bit," using swinging arms to describe somewhere up there and over there. There was no sense questioning my new guide, as I knew I was going, wherever it was. The question was, how long would my aching knee go along? Dodge said it took him a little more than two hours, so it was time to get going. I said a pretty emotional good-bye to Freddie, who was anxious to get back down the mountain. He was a quirky little guy, but he had done a lot to help me down my path, and I didn't know if I would ever see him again. He lit another cigarette and then shuffled off down the road with bow legs and "slippas" on his feet.

I was limping pretty badly when the road got steep again, and it didn't sound like there would be much of a let-up from there on out, but I was determined to get to Picnic if I had to crawl. Little did I know how close I'd come.

We came to a flat spot, where we rested. Dodge lit another spliff, and, after a few tokes off his incredible weed, I lost all interest in my troubles. The pot had a different flavor than any I had ever come across in Northern California. Very spicy. Not sweet-spicy like our Mexican strains or even Thai weed, but an exotic, unfamiliar herb whose attack was most pronounced after exhaling. The trail of smoke off the burning tip of the joint was so comforting that your nose would chase after it. The expansion was slow in coming but grew to the point of bursting on every hit.

"Wow!" I choked. "This is really good!" It continued to expand after I coughed it out. What kind is it?"

"Dis' da' Swaz, mon."

"Swaz," I said. "Never heard of it."

"Ya', mon. Da' Swazi... da' African. It da' only one like it up dis' mountain."

I smoked the roach until it burned my fingers. I had to change shirts, as I was soaking wet from climbing, and at three thousand feet, it was getting cooler out. I pounded down a quart of water and shared some of my mango and papaya, which my body was really hungry for. We spent about half an hour resting on that plateau while Dodge took pleasure in my sincere interest as he described where he was taking me.

"Dis' 'ere herb cyan only come from Jah Valley. Dat' is a hidden valley up dis' mountain only I and I know wyere. I and I fill dis' valley wit' mostly African herbs."

"You filled a valley?" I wanted to get the story straight. "How many plants is that?" Five hundred would have been a lot. I began to calculate, but he interrupted me.

"T'ousand of plants, mon." It tripped out of his mouth like it was nothing.

"I'm sorry?" I asked, "How many?"

"Ya' mon. T'ousand of plants, mon."

"In one place?!" I wasn't whispering any more.

"You see what I'm sayin'. Some o'er 'ere. More o'er dat way. A bunch up 'dere," again with swinging, descriptive arms.

Whatever they yielded, a thousand plants had to be a lot. All of a sudden, my knee wasn't hurting that much anymore, and I was ready to go find this "Jah Valley."

\*  \*  \*  \*  \*  \*  \*

Dodge walked much faster than Freddie, and his strides were huge. I needed a step and a half to his single step, and the difference messed up my rhythm. We rested hardly at all for the next hour-and-a-half, but I could tell I was slowing him down, as he turned many times to wait for me to catch up. Our next rest was taken under a tall jacaranda tree, its great purple flowers back-lit by the promise of a full moon soon to rise over the volcano. The jungle had begun to thin, and taller trees began to dominate the landscape, making it look penetrable, but two steps off the road would land you in jagged lava so treacherous it would destroy a pair of boots in ten minutes. I changed into my third shirt and had to wring out the one I was wearing and hang it from a loop on my pack. An extra pair of socks would have been a good idea, but Freddie hadn't used them, and Dodge must have discarded his a long time ago, having no problem wearing beat-up kicks. My knee was holding up pretty well, considering I'd hauled ass three thousand feet straight up a volcano in the middle of the night. According to my watch, we only had half-an-hour to go, so you'll understand my dismay when Dodge volunteered that we had "only" two more hours to go.

"But you said that an hour-and-a-half ago," I complained.

"For me, ya', mon. I cyan walk up dis' whole mountain and back down in da' time you take to get 'ere," he answered with that reassuring smile. "Don' worry, mon. You gon' make it to da' top."

---

"Well, have we at least made it to the middle of the middle?" I whined like a baby.

But he just laughed. "You come way beyond dat, mon. Dis' more like da' bottom of da' top."

I fiddled with my knee. "I don't know if the body is able, but the spirit is ready to go."

"I *tell* you!" He put the emphasis on "tell." "Dat's how! Wit' dat' attitude you gon' climb da' top dis' mountain," he said, helping me to my feet.

He was very happy with me—why, I'm not sure, as we came from completely different worlds in which there might have been a tendency to mistrust. At that moment, a connection was made, and from then on, he walked beside me, and the conversation we shared made the going much easier. After another hour of hiking, the angle of the road lessened, and we should have been able to move faster but for a new pain growing in the hip of what was my good leg. Dodge must have been annoyed, but showed nothing but concern for my hobbled condition. Just as the road was about to make another steep ascent—which might have led to a complete breakdown on my part—Dodge turned off to our right, and, after wading through twenty feet of tall grass, he ducked through a hole in the barbed-wire fence where the middle strand had been cut. I followed, finding myself on a broken trail through five minutes of tall, dense jungle overgrowth. I was elated to be on level ground and in different terrain. The tangle of branch and vine above my head all but blacked out the glow the moon makes in the sky just as it cracks the horizon, which made it necessary to place my feet very carefully into the flashlight beam. When I came to a small clearing, I found Dodge standing, his back to me, before a huge monolith-like pile of volcanic rock rubble rising forty feet over his head. It was vertical enough that I could reach out and touch it. Although it was as shiny and sharp as new, Dodge said that this flow was hundreds of years old and that this was where it had ended. It just stopped right there, causing a mini-mountain of rubble four-thousand feet above the highway in the middle of the jungle where few people would have even known about it, let alone seen it.

To my amazement, he began to climb the pile by walking across the belly of it. Looking closely with my light, I saw that he followed a path about four inches wide trod by cattle over many years. In places it wasn't the width of a single foot, but using our hands for balance, we scaled that sucker, and once on top, I found myself in a whole new landscape. Dodge's smile broadened across his face like that of someone finally able to reveal a long-held secret. "You see," he said, presenting it to me with an open arm. We stood at the narrow end of the once-cascading lava, where it had had its last drip, ending way up there in jungle obscurity. Above us, the flow widened to sixty feet across, laying waste to everything in between us and the full moon, which now crested the volcano, turning night into near-day. It was like crawling out onto the edge of the moon itself. The lava glistened in its blackness, and nothing dared to grow. To continue climbing, we used a strip of smashed-rock road about six feet wide that ran up the left side of the flow about twenty feet from the jungle's edge. After a short while, as the flow widened, the road went straight up the middle, and by the time we came to our third resting point, I found myself on bald rock in broad moonlight with the whole expanse of the island laid out before me. Over a hundred miles at the shoreline. It was a grand sight, and Dodge was pleased to see my awe. Way to the north, the lights of Kailua-Kona and a couple of big cruise ships in her harbor were the only human stains in sight.

"Is that Kailua?" I asked Dodge, who was concentrating on lighting a five-inch-long, pregnant spliff.

Exhaling a huge cloud, he waved his hand over the tiny eyesore as if casting a spell. The smoke hung around us in the still mountain air. "All Babylon sleep." His low voice emerged from the cloud. It was a simple statement, but it sounded more like prophecy and hinted at the possibility of a life outside of a system that, from this perspective, seemed to flicker in the distance like a desert mirage. Out there on that flow, that calm, quiet moment was the freest I have ever felt. "When Babylon falls, you gonna' be sittin' right 'ere." He looked out over the ocean and took a breath. "Da' birds still gonna' sing, da' fish still gonna' jump da' boat, and da' fruit still gonna' roll up your toe." And as we turned our backs on that churning machine, continuing our climb to the sky, I felt I was making my own personal exodus.

Buoyed by this spiritual nourishment and a growing fascination with my guide, the last half-hour of our climb went quickly and easily. I was in pretty good shape, considering I had climbed nearly five-thousand feet in five hours, when Dodge abruptly stopped and announced with his large grin, "You made it, mon," he extolled, shaking my shoulders and looking into my face with congratulatory eyes. I smiled back at him, trying to catch my breath. Standing straight up, I stretched out to a more erect posture. As I rolled my head, trying to loosen a stiff neck, I took a good look around. I was way out in the middle of fuckin' nowhere.

"Dis' it, mon! Da' top a da' top"

✳    ✳    ✳    ✳    ✳    ✳

My confusion didn't register with Dodge. He seemed like a guy who could never be lost. Turning to the right, he headed off the flow, making a beeline for the jungle. Within a hundred yards, it began to creep over the lava-rock floor. Just a few leafy vines at first, stretching out over the jagged surface, the jungle's never-ending effort to reclaim the scorched earth. Another twenty feet to the tree line, and the lava below our feet disappeared under a thick mat of vegetation, but it was still a most uneven surface, making it difficult to maintain balance. Dodge was much more spry on this terrain. He stopped here and there to point out small lava tubes hiding under the mat, who-knows-how-deep and just wide enough to suck in an unfortunate leg. In minutes, we were ensconced in deep jungle forest. The way Dodge traveled around and through the trees and up the occasional creek bed made it difficult to keep up and the artificial darkness had me wondering what I would do if I should get lost in that wilderness. At one point, he got ahead enough for me to miss a few turns, and, before he knew it, I was all alone. I tried to find my own way for a few minutes, but, realizing that I was getting myself hopelessly entangled, I decided to sit down and smoke a joint that Ruben had given me, until Dodge found me only moments later. We forged into the forest for three-quarters of an hour, leaving the flow and my entire world behind. As the first hint of dawn lit our way, my guide slowed to the pace of a hunter stalking prey. "We're 'ere," he whispered. I didn't know where "here" was, but I was glad to be near the end, for my body possessed no more strength or brain chemicals that would pass for strength. As the light slowly increased, I noticed the shapes of the trees surrounding me, standing fifteen to twenty feet tall and looking strangely familiar. With symmetrical branches off a single stalk and long, flat, seven-fingered, leaves with serrated edges. Their numbers increased as we continued, and, for a moment, my heart pumped newfound adrenaline, and my mind threatened to overload on dollar signs and zeros. A thousand of these monsters would be some kinda' record. When I asked Dodge, he had trouble containing his laughter, muffling his mouth with his arm. And then he informed me that this was the "hapu'u" fern. "Plentiful, but it don' smoke too well." Finally, he came to the edge of a small downslope that overlooked a little valley only a quarter-mile wide and narrowed at the top and bottom, diamond-like. He rested on one knee, and, in that low tone of voice that accented all things mystical, he said, "Jah Valley!"

As we descended into it, Dodge began to describe it. It was about a mile long and had been left there by an ancient flow that went "dis' way an dat' way an' left a "puka," (a hole,) in between. The

denseness of its forest was half that of the surrounding flow, but
Dodge assured me that they had filled the extra space with plenty of
those Swazi lung-busters. He began to point them out. A few here
and there where small trees provided the perfect cover.

Walking deeper into the valley, small signs of human habitation
became evident. The carpet-like mesh of vegetation was well trampled,
leaving criss-crossing trails running in all directions, like the spokes of
a wheel, and we neared the hub. The terrain opened up into relatively
flat, meadow-like pockets divided by large, arroyo outcroppings of
black rock. Then we rounded one such wall and came abruptly upon
their camp. Two more Rastas were outside a crude but large tent made
from three big, green Visqueen tarps strung from the arroyo top to
the valley floor and propped up by wooden poles in the middle. They
created a kind of three-room lean-to, up to eight feet in the middle
and sloping to the ground at weird angles like a Turkish tent. In this
way, it clung close to the ground and blended into the contours of
the flow. One gentleman wore green, boot-cut khakis that looked too
short for his severely worn, leather, closed-toed sandals and ragged,
sleeveless tee-shirt. He had a steaming coffee mug in one hand, and
the other was jammed into his pocket with his shoulders hunched up
around his ears from the cold. He stood next to a similarly disheveled
compatriot in shorts and a many-pocketed, beige vest that looked like
one you might go fishing in but was probably military surplus. He was
squatting with his butt on his heels, huddling with a second mug in
an attempt to corral the maximum amount of warmth.

\*    \*    \*    \*    \*    \*    \*

Russell and Charles looked like they had been in the bush a long
time. Besides their unkempt appearance, the camp also looked well
lived-in. Empty bottles and cans dotted the area, and piles of refuse
for burning marred the otherwise natural landscape. Garden supplies

like plastic pipe, one-gallon black-plastic grow bags, buckets, and bags of topsoil, which they had carried up the volcano, were strewn all over. They were friendly enough, offering me coffee, though I felt they were suspicious of my motives. After all, this was their domain. A place no Hawaiians and only a few motivated hippies would bother to climb to. Still, they offered me a white, plastic bucket for a seat and a breakfast of peanut butter and jelly sandwiches, which tasted like a gourmet meal after the long hike up there. The tent doubled as living quarters and drying shed. No plants were hanging, but there were three propane heaters, big, metal jobs they had lugged up the mountain to warm the cool, high-altitude air. After we ate, they lit up another one of the now-familiar spliffs, and we talked awhile, but they never asked why I was there. Each of them in turn puffed a cloud of smoke behind which his face disappeared, without a discernable effect, but when the six-inch-long quarter-ounce joint came my way, I took a lungful and waited for the explosion. It went in smooth as water and tasted like a field of spice, but didn't start to expand until after I exhaled. As the smoke poured out, the taste filled my mouth from way in the back. A hashy taste I recognized as the taste of trichomes burning, but with a unique lip-smacking richness. The ache in my lungs grew from imperceptible to overwhelming as each second passed, and, eventually, I began to cough. Slowly at first, then uncontrollably, until I thought I would lose my PB&Js. A punishing blow to the solar plexus. Shortly thereafter, the shockwave hit my brain like a psychedelic concussion. A congratulatory chuckle passed between them when they saw how their weed had wrecked me. I laughed, too, as I wiped the drool from the corners of my mouth. "Wo-ow!" I gasped, trying to speak before my lungs were ready to let air pass. My inability to talk made them fall into hysterics, and we all had a great crack-up. It lasted long after we had forgotten what started it and left the four of us struggling for a breath. "Wow!" I tried to continue, still unsure of my wind.

"I tell you!" Dodge said.

"Yes I!" Russell agreed.

"Thanks and praises!" Charles said, as he wiped a tear from his right eye.

By nine, my three friends were having a nice morning beer and discussing their day's work. Though they were equal partners, Dodge was giving most of the direction and handing out the day's chores. Most of these had to do with filling said gallon bags with said soil mixture and finding new places up valley to put them. Then finding uphill water by damming up whatever trickles they could uncover. They had to have another two hundred spots for the starts he said would soon be ready to transplant from their greenhouse. That, he explained, was where we would find the illusive Picnic, whose job was to raise these starts from seed and grow them up to about a foot tall, a crucial task. He stayed by himself in a small, secondary camp down valley that served as a nursery.

It took less than ten minutes to walk there on one of the down-valley foot trails that ran over the jungle-covered flow, its jagged terrain replete with nooks and crannies perfect for hiding four-footers in one-gallon bags of dirt.

He was sitting up in his bed, a backpacker's two-inch-thick air mattress with a beat-up mummy bag pulled down around his waist and a four-inch roach balanced on his lip, just like Dodge's. His pillow, laid against a stack of twenty-pound sacks of topsoil, made a comfortable back rest from which he had a great downhill view. He rose a minute for me to introduce myself as Chet's emissary, accepted the medallion, and then bade me to sit down on the foot of his cushion. He was the exact opposite of what I had expected. To my surprise, he was shorter than I, at about five-foot-eight, and slight. Two belt loops on his right hip tied together with twine served as the belt necessary for holding up a ragged, blue pair of Big Ben painter's pants. His gray, hooded sweatshirt bore the logo of the University of Hawaii, where, he told me later, he had studied horticulture. His skin was dark brown, making the white ovals of his translucent, black eyes peek out of the darkness of his face. Unruly foot-long dreadlocks, black and thick, often got in the way of his face, until he took a handful on each side and tied them together in the back. His small hands were creased and calloused at the palm, like those of a day laborer, with short, strong fingers. I told him about the jam we were in, and, though I couldn't see how he could help, I gave him Chet's message. Simply, "Come home," and that was enough. He didn't have any questions or want to know the details.

He spoke to me in a voice as cool and smooth as river rock, in the manner of old friends long separated. Quietly and slowly. "I bin' dis' bumble clot jungle twenty mont's now, my brudda'. In dat' time, only twice been down da 'mountain," he said, "and I no come down twenty more 'cept for his call." He produced a small, black jewel case from a backpack standing upright beside his bed that contained a blue ribbon with white stars at the throat. Dangling from the ribbon was a gold eagle perched on a bar, engraved with the word "Valor." Picnic reattached the gold star to the bar with two gold chain links, squeezed them together with his teeth, and then returned the Medal of Honor to its case.

Many people might have other questions to ask this mystery man. Me? I stayed true to color. "What do you do with all this weed?" I asked.

"Oh, me bredren always tyke cyre' dis." He brushed the silly question away with the flick of his wrist.

"Cannot spend dis' kind of money up here, mon," I quipped in an ill-attempted half-patois that I subconsciously slipped into whenever I was in a group of people who spoke a foreign tongue.

"Money," he scoffed. "Amazing da' way dat' money cyan' come to such a one who cyan' cyre' less." He held his fingertips to his chest in a humbling gesture. "I got bags a dis' money everybody so eager to 'ave, gon' to rot in di's 'ere jungle, mon."

A smile crept onto his face as he got up and walked the few steps to a corner opening in the thirty-square-foot, fully-enclosed lean-to he slept beside. Lifting the flap a little, he peeked inside and then back at me, still smiling, and said, "Come see da ladies in my life." Then he disappeared into the tent. Of course, if you know me by now, you know that I followed without hesitation. I kicked my way through the clutter of garbage strewn about, and then passed through the threshold of Picnic's temple nursery. Three-tiered platforms of wood were separated by a path in the middle so he could easily tend the rows of starters that stretched the length of the tent. About five hundred of them in every stage, from sprouts to stout one-footers ready to transplant. I helped Picnic lift the roof off the top, allowing the girls to taste their first drop of morning sunlight causing them to lift their leaves and to go to work. Unlike the filthy campsite, this part of the project was immaculate. No garbage, no dirt even. All the cups of sprouted ganja were carefully arranged by size and strain. Each plant was perfect, with very few stragglers. It was apparent that someone was taking conscious care here. It meant a lot to somebody, and that somebody was Picnic. So I praised him. "These are so beautiful. They are obviously well loved."

"Dis' da' herb dat' speaks da' word, mon." He spoke in the same profound manner as had Dodge. In fact, he seemed to share not only Dodge's look, but many of his mannerisms. "Da' word is a trut' dat' is 'ard to 'ere, a taste dat' is 'ard to touch, a smell dat' is 'ard to see. But 'dere is magic in da' word an da' herb release da' magic."

"Wiser words were never spoken," I said, my heart reeling from the plain truth of it.

"Da' prophet once say, 'Dem' say wit' age comet' wisdom, but 'dere's a natural mystic floatin' tru' da' air,'" he said, quoting Bob Marley. Relighting the spliff, he exhaled over his "ladies," just as I had in my garden.

"So many of them," I said, amazed.

"Yes, I. The coli mus' burn!" he exclaimed. "Every day I plant da' seed, mon."

"Every day?" I asked

"Ya', mon. In Hawaii cyan' plant any time da' year," he said.

"Where do you put them all?" I asked.

"Put dem' is not da' problem, mon," he said. "Problem is how to start enough to put everywyere'. I and i mus' fill d's' shed forty times each year."

"Just how many of these things do you have in this valley?" I wondered aloud.

"From bottom to top, roughly twenty t'ousand," he said calmly.

"Twenty thousand!!?" I all but yelled. "My god! Twenty thousand?!"

"Ya', mon." He smiled again at my surprise, choking slightly on the smoke.

"What's your average yield per plant?" I asked, getting right down to business.

"Round quarter to half, mon," he said matter-of-factly.

But my Narrator was spinning numbers. Twenty thousand quarter-pounds is five-thousand pounds! "Holy shit!" I said. "Five-thousand pounds?"

"No, no, my brudda'. Quarter to half *ounce*," he laughed.

"Oh," I said, almost relieved. I quickly recalculated the total yield. "Three-hundred pounds. Wow! That's still really good."

"Ya', mon. Jah bless," he said sincerely.

I examined his "ladies" for an hour or so while he watered and fertilized. Then I helped him plant six flats of newly germinated seeds. By eleven a.m., the sun was heating up the valley, and a mist rose smelling of sticky pot. Picnic tied on a pair of tan, Payless work boots that had clearly paid a price for this jungle life and took me on a two-hour tour of his extensive garden. He was very proud of their work and, seeing my enthusiasm, was eager to show me all the tricks of his trade. The whole time keeping those wicked fire-sticks burning. The plants were lanky, two-to-three-foot jobbers with few lateral branches and sparse growth. They were planted in the one-gallon bags and looked pretty weather-tortured. They yielded several four-inch buds completely covered with unusually long white stamens and some airy fluff down low. But there were ten thousand females! That's thousand with a *th*!" By midday, the sun and the weed were too strong to continue. After checking on the nursery, we retired to the shade of their Turk-ish tent, where I passed out for a few hours on one of those tiny, folding, beach chairs. It was not a fitful or comatose sleep. Rather a dream of dreams. Of altogetherness, represented by a flower that grew freely around every bend of my imagination.

✻ ✻ ✻ ✻ ✻ ✻ ✻

Back in San Francisco, Detectives Kassen and Nolan were reviewing their upcoming indictments with U.S. Assistant District Attorney Frank Simmons, the man who would prosecute the case. Simmons was a D.A. they had worked with successfully many times before. He was exacting and precise when it came to the question of whether or not there was enough evidence to charge and convict suspects, but once he felt the police had done their job, he prosecuted relentlessly in the name of an outraged community. And of these convictions he was certain. He had Patrick and me dead to rights. Patrick's pop would surely go down as well. The only problem was this fellow "Chet" whom Patrick had identified as the ringleader. The one who knew where the money was. He would have to be brought to justice before they could charge the others. Kassen and Nolan were happy with that. They knew they had three down, and they had every intention of getting the fourth.

✻ ✻ ✻ ✻ ✻ ✻ ✻

It wasn't so much the loud reggae music that woke me as the scratchy hissing of the cassette tape coming out of a beat-up boom box with one blown speaker. But the low-fi of the sound quality didn't stop my four comrades from enjoying Bob Marley's "Rebel Music" and dancing slightly hunched over in the tent. My eyes opened separately, and the fIrst thing I felt was the thunderous pain in my calves and thighs. The others noticed I was awake and e xtolled me to join in the revelry. They each held a can of beer, and it looked as though these hadn't been the first of the evening. They had had plenty of them, each one carried on foot to this high place. Something no backpacker in his right mind would do. I guess you've got to have your priorities. The smells coming from the camp stove on the other side of the tent were strange and inviting. Just as I regained my senses, they came again with the herb, insisting that it was the necessary precursor to any good meal. And the food was good, too, unlike anything I had ever had, mainly due to the assortment of spices. The dishes were well spiced, to say the least. The fIrst pot was jasmine rice with a little cut-up breadfruit and papaya cooked in. Spiced with cumin, cardamom, and turmeric. The second, a lentil dish with potatoes and green beans, was hopped up on generous amounts of garlic and those little, red, Hawaiian hot peppers I was beginning to love. Both put a whuppin' on my taste buds and made me think how little I knew about spice. We shared an after-dinner spliff, and I even joined them in a couple of beers. Two were my limit, but that didn't slow them down. They turned the music back up and did that cool reggae dance that I, as a white guy, cannot genetically do. Nevertheless, they got me up to try, and we all got a good laugh from the sight. Each in turn got up to do his impression of my reggae stylin' every time the laughter subsided. When no more could be squeezed out of that, they recounted for Picnic the story of my first big pull off the Swazi when I had just reached camp. One, then another, hit the joint, and then they started coughing with great theatrics, and gasped out the word, "Wo...ow!" followed by much knee slapping and floor rolling. Even when there was nothing left to laugh at, they continued. I asked what was so funny? Dodge clued me in. "We jus' laugh," he said. And we did. I swear, I laughed until I thought my ribs would pop out.

Right around the time when I thought I was inebriated enough to puke, whacked enough to pass out and sore enough to fall over, Picnic announced that it was time to go back down the "hill." I struggled to pull myself together while he said good-bye to these brothers who had kept him safe from harm. He promised to return soon, but they worried what would become of him "in the hands of Babylon." There were many salutations of loyalty, respect and righteousness. Much hugging, hand shaking and back slapping. My shirts had dried during the day, but my lava-lacerated shoes needed to be repaired with duct tape. I wasn't really sure that my body could take the trip back down so soon, but, happily, my knees didn't hurt near as bad as my thighs, and I took that as a good sign.

About fifteen minutes out of camp, we heard the egg-beater rumble of helicopters coming our way. Picnic stopped to search the sky, then continued out of the valley at a quickened pace. We had to get into thicker jungle, or we'd be sitting ducks. I tripped several times, scratching my hands and knees, as I kept an eye on the sky. My heart rate jumped as the choppers got closer. Something stuck in my throat made it difficult to swallow. We climbed out of the valley and dove into the thicket just as the helicopters passed over our heads and into Jah Valley behind us. I dug in to a lava crevice at the foot of a big hapu'u fern. I remained perfectly still as the copters doubled back, but my heart rate was cranked up to faint. I tried to remain calm, and though I wasn't screaming and running, I was sweating like a thoroughbred and shaking fitfully. Picnic was barely hidden among the tall tropical flowers at the edge of the valley, watching. No fewer than eight of those black "birds" began to criss-cross the mountainside, grid-like, searching for the dreaded "pakalolo," but within moments, Picnic began to smile. "Look," he said, "Jah bring da fog." Sure enough, a thick fog rolled over the mountain and poured into the valley, filling it to the brim and then whiting out the whole mountain. The choppers had to bug out. Picnic laughed loudly as he helped me out of my rabbit hole. "Babylon try to bring clot', mon, but Jah bless." I must have looked like I was in shock. "You Jah soldier now, mon!" he said between chuckles. "Ya', mon! In Jah army of righteousness!" He laughed and praised Jah all the way back to the bald flow that would lead us back to civilization.

He moved very quickly down the lava, stopping only once when the fog broke to smoke and enjoy the colors in the sky. Then off we went, in flash-lit darkness, barely rested. My muscles were well oiled, and I was moving easily for about an hour, but after we climbed down the end of the flow and hit the dirt/rock road, Picnic took off downhill at a "jog" that had me near all-out running to keep up. What had taken me six hours to climb took only two-and-a-half hours to descend. A literally blistering pace that I would have to pay for.

\*　　\*　　\*　　\*　　\*　　\*　　\*

When we got to the highway, we had to wait fifteen minutes for Freddie to get there in his truck. It was just after ten at night, and he took us right back to the beach in "I Won't Say" village, where Albert and Ruben would once again be my hosts. I stumbled the whole way down the king's trail to the beach, where I collapsed under a coconut palm tree. Picnic was greeted warmly by the brothers and the others in the community, and then they disappeared into the shack. I scoured the beach for Alana. She was in front of a hut at the back end of the beach, working on necklaces of shells and semi-precious stones that she sold by the wharf where I first met Freddie. She came to assist me when she saw me limping toward her. She helped me into a large nearby hammock and got me a pillow. Just before I fell asleep, she kissed me. One steamy kiss. All lips, but hot.

The next day, she started me on a program of Lomi Lomi massage, long swims, and healthy food that lasted five days until Picnic and I returned to the mainland. We spent the days together and the nights around the big campfire "talking story" with the others. Every night, Picnic broke out his duffel bag stuffed with a couple pounds of his best, which he called the "top da' crop," to the great joy of his Hawaiian family. Reuben and I examined the whole bag. Light green buds of incredible density. Hard-rock marijuana. Not huge, but as sugar-coated as Frosted Flakes. He looked around the beach, appreciating the beauty, as he practically inhaled the sticky bud through his great nostrils. Putting his club of an arm around my neck and giving me a good shake, he said, "Is dis' you, Boo? Why you come stay go? Dis' is you, Boo."

"Yes, Boule, this is me," I had to agree.

"Is what is, bra," he observed. Then we shared the herb, bonding over the holy smoke. Picnic lavished me with the stuff, giving me a handful every morning before Alana and I went for our daily trek.

The morning after our return, I got my first look at the chameleon. Yes, something about him was different. It was subtle and took a while to register, but it was undeniably there. The once-black pupils of his eyes had turned a lustrous golden brown. He seemed a little uncomfortable in his own skin. His stubby, muscular fingers became longer and more slender. The calluses of his palms were melting away. It was eerie for me, and although he knew it would happen, it must have scared him some. By the second morning, in place of long dreadlocks, his hair was chopped shoulder-length and curly, and it had lost the black sheen and become a dark ash color. His very skin was changing, as well. Gone was the smooth, dark, chocolate color. Now blotchy patches in lighter shades of brown pockmarked his face.

On the sixth day, we prepared to leave the island. Alana and I had become very close, and I had almost forgotten the troubles waiting for me back in California. Our days were filled with much kissing and tender touching, but no more. That's it, until that last kiss. The good-bye kiss that says "return soon." With one arm crooked around my neck, she kissed me hard with an insistent tongue, then grabbed my dick firmly in her fist and pulled me right up against her belly. This stirred a hunger in me that has not yet subsided. As the embrace ended, she whispered in my ear, "Come back to me." Knowing my future was not my own, I only nodded.

I waited for Picnic where the beach met the trail, but I couldn't believe it when a complete stranger approached. He had changed into a tank top with a surfing scene, knee-length swim shorts, and sandals. His hair, now as brown as mine, was shorter still, cut in a shaggy manner around his face. Where there had been a beard, patchy facial hair gave way to skin almost the color of Albert's and Ruben's. He could easily have been a local. My surprise would have been shock if I hadn't witnessed the change. Still, my chin was agape, my eyes fixed on the miracle. He chuckled at my reaction. No longer disoriented, he had a certain resigned amusement about him. He was his happiest—his most kind and real—as a Rasta in the jungle, but he was also the best kind of friend, the kind that comes running.

# CHAPTER 19

It was seven-thirty the following Monday morning, only a weekend and thirty hours of catch-up sleep since I dropped Picnic off, when the phone in my trampy Motel 6 room awakened me, sounding like church bells in a dream. It was Chet, and he wanted me to meet him in half an hour at a little coffee house not far from where I was staying. Given my still-recovering condition, I would have driven the two blocks, but the cops still had my money-laden Mobile Hilton impounded, with little hope for her return. When I reached the "Dig Inn," Chet was already seated at a corner table with another well-dressed man I didn't recognize but knew to be Picnic reincarnated. He wore a black suit with a white shirt and black tie. His hair, now dirty blond and straight, was cut short, and his eyes as crystal blue as an alpine lake. Under the table, the outfit was finished off with the same patent-leather shoes worn by every cop since the beginning of time.

Chet beckoned me to sit across from them. "Hey, pal, welcome back to the world."

"Yeah, it took me two full days to come to," I said.

"I want you to meet Lieutenant Colonel Glen Edwards," he said, referring to Picnic as if I had never seen him before. Colonel Edwards was gobbling bacon and hash browns, a far cry from the healthy delights we had shared in the jungle, but he nodded in my direction and gave my outstretched hand one firm shake. His once-stubby fingers were long and slender now and the palm as smooth as a chief executive officer's. "What'll you have?" Chet asked, offering me a menu.

"I'd like a get-out-of-jail-free card and three million dollars for passing Go." I wasn't going to let Chet forget what he had promised me. No charges had yet been filed against me in the months since the bust, but my lawyer felt there would be. Rather than push to find out their intention, she said it would be better to wait them out, so it was up to Chet to make something happen.

"Today is the day Colonel Edwards goes to work," he said excitedly. "He's going to give them a story that'll get the whole hive buzzing." I looked at Picnic for a reaction, but he never looked up from his plate. There was no love coming from him. No positive feeling like before. Just cold closedness. "I expect they'll be getting in touch with your lawyer soon thereafter to haul you in for more questions. They'll be trying to figure out what the fuck hit 'em. I want you to make them think you are cooperating by telling them what you know. And that is that you were hired by Patrick Halston and his dad. That the only other person involved, to your knowledge, was a helper hired by you for menial labor, whose name you will not reveal. And that you were not paid commensurate with the amount of weed you grew. Patrick was the only one to take weed out of the building, and he paid you an agreed-upon salary. You never saw the bulk of the money or knew where it went. Period! You were a hired gun employed solely for the purpose of increasing the yield on their already-established grow. No more! They'll keep pushing, but you can't tell them what you don't know. Right?"

"If you say so." I was still unsure. Feeling like a pawn in Chet's game. "What is the rest of the story?"

"Never mind that. The less you know, the better. Just trust me." I'd heard that before, and it was getting harder to do as time passed, but he obviously had something going, so I was compelled to go along.

I hadn't even gotten my meal when they got up to depart. Chet threw a folded twenty on the table. "It's on me," he said as they headed for the door. I walked them to the street, where Colonel Edwards put on a pair of mirrored sunglasses that blacked out his eyes and seemed to suck out all the light rather than reflect it. They got into a parked Polaris that was so dark blue it was almost black. Edwards jammed the transmission into gear and tore away from the sidewalk like a seasoned cop. No longer the dread-locked, dark-skinned, dirty Rasta I had abducted from the jungle only a few days before.

✳   ✳   ✳   ✳   ✳   ✳   ✳

United States Assistant District Attorney Frank Simmons barely had time to hang his coat on the hook-stand by the door, and the intercom was already buzzing. The dry, crackled voice of his secretary informed him that his nine o'clock was waiting. He glanced around the small office to make sure that all was in perfect order. "All right then, let's get started."

Frank Simmons was a company man, but his company was the U.S. of A., and he had made a career of it. Eight years in the Marine Corps, ending with a tour in Vietnam just as the war was getting started. He saw what had happened to the French and felt from the beginning that the only way to win was to go all out, right from the start. By '65, he knew it wasn't going to happen that way and so decided not to re-up. After three years of law school and studying to pass the bar, he signed on with the Justice Department, where he put away bad guys for eighteen years. He was a go-by-the-book kind of guy who was not prepared for the kind of moral conundrum that Colonel Edwards was bringing through his door.

Picnic came into the room with a thin, black, Zero Halliburton briefcase in one hand and his credentials in the other.

"Ah, District Attorney Simmons. I'm Colonel Glen Edwards with the National Security Agency. It's good of you to make time for me." Picnic knew this Assistant D.A. would have to make time for a liaison from the N.S.A., but he wanted to humor him. Simmons inspected the identification and found it in order. After introductions and a hand shake resembling two sides of a vice, Picnic sat down in front of Simmons's desk and placed the case in the adjacent chair.

"Call me Frank. What can we do for you?" Simmons asked, retrieving his own chair.

"Frank, the N.S.A. needs your help with a small problem of national security." Picnic knew instinctually how to spin it. "It seems that you gentlemen have snagged a couple of our operatives in a recent bust you conducted."

"Is that right?" Simmons answered.

"Yes, sir." Picnic kept a respectful tone.

"What bust is that?" Simmons wondered where this was going.

"Well, it's that big, indoor pot farm in a mill up in the Sierra foothills."

"Yeah, yeah," Simmons broke in. "What, one of your boys got caught up in that mess?"

"Well, sir, the N.S.A. is inextricably connected to this project and to the men you are getting ready to indict." Picnic opened the briefcase and handed the D.A. several eight-by-ten, black-and-white pictures of the mill, the gardens in full swing, and, finally, a graying older man in a marine uniform with plenty of ribbons decorating his chest. "This man is retired Marine Corps Colonel Leonard Halston. He has worked on many special operations with the Agency and is a patriot and servant of our great country. Unfortunately, as you know, he is also the owner of the facility in question."

Simmons recognized the picture at once. "Yeah, we are investigating him. So this is one of your guys doing a little something on the side? I don't see why he shouldn't go down like all the rest of the hippies growing dope when they know it's against the law." Simmons wasn't impressed so far.

"It's a bit more complicated than that." Special Agent Edwards retrieved the pictures and snapped the case closed. Folding his hands in his lap, he paused for several beats. "Frank, for reasons of national security, I can't explain further. The simple fact is, if you take the colonel down, he is going to cause way more trouble for U.S. foreign relations than he is worth. If you charge him, the government would be forced to spill the beans about its illegal activities, making a conviction nearly impossible. Between you and me, brother, he is one of us. I know if we work together on this, we can work something out that is mutually beneficial."

"Baloney!" Simmons barked. "Probably the single largest indoor growing operation in recorded history and you want me to can the whole thing!? With no explanation! I won't do it!" If this guy thought he was going to shelve the whole matter, he had another thing coming.

Edwards had expected as much, and, without an argument, he rose to his feet with his briefcase and extended his hand politely. "I'll relay your words to my superiors. They will be disappointed. They had hoped you would make this easy."

D. A. Simmons met the handshake reflexively, not sure if he had just been threatened. He felt flushed and was angry that his visitor hadn't even cracked a sweat.

After Edwards left his office, Simmons began at once to contact the National Security Agency to check out the story. Of course, no one would answer his questions or confirm or deny anything. Except that they were very interested in Colonel Edwards and wanted to speak to him right away, thereby confirming that he was a valued operative. Simmons's next call was to an outraged Kassen and Nolan.

\* \* \* \* \* \* \*

When I checked in with my lawyer that evening, she was a bit frantic. She told me that Officer Kassen had called repeatedly and wanted to see me down at the federal building... "yesterday!" I was impressed with how soon Chet's prediction had come about. Hopefully, his guarantee would prove equally good.

This time they put me in a room with real walls. All walls with no windows, just wooden chairs and table and a desk light. I told my lawyer to wait outside in case I needed her, because I thought I might have to answer a few questions, and I knew she would advise against it. Kassen was dressed in a very expensive-looking, dark-brown, single-breasted Italian suit. The jacket was cut in a style befitting a gentleman, the pants perfectly pressed. But he was just short of fuming and snorting when the door closed behind me, and Nolan was already trying to hold him back. "So, yer' some kinda secret agent," he blurted out. I didn't have to act to give him my most confused look. "Don't gimme' that face," he yelled. Then in a whisper that drove spittle between his teeth, "Listen, you little shit!" He got right up in my face. "There's no way yer' gettin' out of this! N.S.A. or no! Now, tell me, who is this Chester Hawthorne, and where can I find him?" Right back to loud and intimidating, just shy of shouting. "Who did you sell the dope to, and where the fuck is the money!?"

"I told you before, there is only one guy you didn't get, and he was just a day laborer. I'm not going to give him to you. As for the money... I never took pound one out of that box."

"I don't believe that for a minute," Kassen snapped.

"Hey, I'm trying to cooperate with you. I want out of this mess." I played my part. "I could call in that lawyer out there, and you know what her advice would be." Kassen was furious. He grabbed the collar of my jacket and popped me a good one right on the left side of my face. Then he looked over at his partner. "He swung at me!" Kassen lied. "You saw it!" He retrained his eyes on mine. "Yer' tryin' to feed me that tired line of bullshit! You were just some kinda' employee." The brute couldn't pull off the subtlety of sarcasm. Nolan pulled him off me, but it took a minute to shake the stars.

"Yes, that exactly. Patrick hired me and paid me a monthly salary. It couldn't have been more than two percent. He took all the weed, and I never saw it after it was dry enough to put in a bag." I was more insistent and combative. I could feel my cheekbone swelling.

"This little shit is dirty!" Kassen pleaded with Nolan, as the latter restrained him.

"Kase, he checks out, man," Nolan implored his out-of-control partner. "Sure, he's dirty, but we don't decide who goes down and who doesn't."

"Bullshit!" Kassen yelled. "This guy is goin' down right now!" He grabbed me by the collar of my shirt and the back of my belt and started shoving me through the door.

"What for?" I yelled, trying to get the lawyer to jump in as we blew by.

"Assaulting an officer!" he yelled back, looking sideways at his partner, who rolled his eyes and said nothing. Back into the slammer I went again.

Less than an hour later, I was returned to the interrogation room. Agent "Wild Bill" Kassen was still at the peak of his anger. He growled at me through gritted teeth. "If you're gonna get outta here, there's only one way yer' gonna do it." He picked up the old-style desk phone, turned it to face me, and slammed it back down on the desk with a ring. Pushing the handle into my face, he demanded, "I want this Chester Hawthorne dude's head on a plate! And if I don't get it, yer' ass is goin' down instead, boy! Mark my words! I don't give a damn what those Washington suits say!"

This was my moment, and I knew it. Chet had said it would come, and now I had to play it through. I let the tears I'd held back for so long well up in my eyes and looked away from his threatening face. "I can't," I said weakly.

"Sure you can," Kassen grinned, sensing that I was broken. "It's your choice, brother. I can't see you doin' twenty years for anyone."

He pushed the receiver at me again. I slowly reached out for it but didn't take it. "If I help you... I walk? Free? No tail?" A little anger trailed into my voice.

"We take this guy down, and you testify against him, if necessary, then you walk," he shot back with self-satisfaction, knowing I was probably going to walk anyway.

I took the phone. As I dialed, Agent Nolan took down the number and listened in on a second line. It was the only number I'd had for Chet since his reappearance, and my two new friends were quite surprised when the operator answered on the other end, "United States Pentagon. Good afternoon, Colonel Hawthorne's office. How may I help you?"

The looks on their faces were priceless. "Is he in?" I knew he wasn't. It was just a service operator.

"Colonel Hawthorne is not available. Can I take a message?"

"Yes, please tell him that Jason wants to see him." I wasn't sure where this was going.

"One moment, please," she said. The cops and I waited a solid five minutes for an answer. Only moments earlier, they had been slobbering over themselves with glee at the prospect of bringing in a big fish. Now their faces showed only shock and doubt. They hammered me with questions until the operator finally returned. "Mr. Jason?"

"Yes, ma'am?" I wondered.

"The colonel would like you to meet him at zero nine hundred hours tomorrow at the following address." I looked over at Nolan as he scribbled the information down on the pad. "Can I tell him you will be there?" He nodded his approval, and I told her I'd be there. "Thank you, Mr. Jason, I'll tell the colonel. Good day, sir."

\*    \*    \*    \*    \*    \*    \*

The next morning, Assistant District Attorney Simmons was intercepted by two, large, burly men in impeccable black suits and white shirts in the garage of the federal building as he exited his car. As if the radio wires in their ears and patented spook glasses hadn't already identified them, they each produced N.S.A. badges from clips on their belts, casually allowing their long-barreled side-arms to swing menacingly into view. He immediately surmised that they were the follow-up to the visit from Colonel Edwards.

"A.D.A. Simmons," the goon on his left stated.

"Who are you?" Simmons shot back defensively.

"I'm Colby, and this is Peterson. We work under General Quinn at the National Security Agency. He sent us to get you."

"To get me!" the D.A. snapped.

"Yes, to bring you to a secure location," Colby answered.

Simmons didn't like the sound of it. "A secure location?" he asked, thinking, secure for whom.

"Yes, sir. He said he would like to engage you in a frank discussion regarding an issue vital to national security." Colby parroted the general's words.

"Tell him to come to my office. I'm not going anywhere with you." The D.A. tried to retake control of the situation.

"I'm sorry, sir. I'm afraid we have to insist." Agent Peterson moved around the D.A.'s right side.

"Do you know who you are threatening!?" He tried again to assert himself, to no effect.

"Don't mean to threaten, sir, but we have our orders, and there is no getting around that," Agent Colby replied. Just then a thirty-foot limousine swung into their aisle, the tires screeching on the polished cement floor of the garage. Seeing no option, Simmons climbed into the back of the limo, facing forward.

The two N.S.A. agents followed, sitting in the opposite seats, facing Simmons. The passenger compartment was illuminated by a dozen or so running lights tucked neatly into the upholstery. The windows were darkened to black. A.D.A Simmons had no idea where he was going. Not even a direction. This made for an uncomfortable ride, but only a few minutes later, they pulled into the giant, roll-up door of a large warehouse somewhere near the Oakland Army Base.

Even through overcast skies, sunlight entering the roll-up door reflected on the concrete floor where water gathered by the drains. It left shadows to the left and right, making Simmons more uneasy as he got out of the long car. Crates and palletted boxes sealed in cellophane shrink-wrap lined the edges of this tunnel of light and rose into darkness above. He brushed the wrinkles from his pants and straightened his tie and collar as though this might straighten his nerve and strengthen his resolve not to buckle under political pressure.

A figure appeared from the rows of crates ahead of the parked limo and hurriedly crossed the warehouse floor, the leather soles of his shoes leaving a little shimmering zigzag trail of mirrors where he tracked through a water puddle. As he came more into the light, his long shadow gave way to a much smaller man. His suit, tailored sharply at the waist, revealed his somewhat narrow stature. He was about five-foot-five and 145 pounds. His crisp, white hat and dark-blue, buttoned-down uniform with bars on his shoulder signified his rank as captain in the U.S Navy. His demeanor matched his size. With shoulders raised up near his ears and back slumped forward, he looked up through classic, Coke-bottle glasses, as he approached the A.D.A. with his right hand extended. Simmons met him in front of the car with a stiff handshake and felt the surrender of a weak arm that he had always believed was a sign of a lack of confidence.

"Assistant District Attorney Simmons, glad you could join us," said the man through a weaselly grin, never offering his own name. "The general will be glad to see you."

"Am I to take it that I'm your guest here?" the A.D.A. asked sarcastically.

"Why, certainly, sir. By invitation of General Quinn and under his protection." Was this weak-wristed weasel trying to reassure him or subtly threaten? "You're perfectly secure in here, sir."

Simmons decided to ignore the comment and continued to question. "What is this place?" he asked, looking beyond his host and standing his tallest to amplify their difference in stature.

"This is just a collection and trans-shipment point for international cargo that we, your government, have coming and going."

"For Central and South America?" the A.D.A. butted in.

The Navy man started to back away, motioning for Simmons to follow him as he retreated down the same, darkened aisle he had come from. "Yes, well, as you might know or guess, it is sometimes necessary for the government to maintain certain off-record facilities in support of U.S. national security," he said without the slightest trace of smugness. Simmons nervously followed his host, glancing from side to side for danger coming out of the dark. He relaxed a little when a glance over his shoulder confirmed that the two, huge, suited goons were not following. Maybe he could just walk out of there. He entertained the idea for a moment, but adrenaline-laced curiosity propelled him into an uncertain future.

Exiting the warehouse through steel double doors, he entered a fluorescently lit hallway with windows to the left and right that peered into smallish and otherwise windowless offices, each one occupied by uniformed military personnel buzzing in and out like bees in a honey-comb hotel. The weasel continued through the door at the opposite end of the hall without acknowledging those he passed along the way. When Simmons breached the doorway, the light changed to a gentle white, illuminating plush, blue carpets and upscale appointments like those of a Wall Street brokerage. Original paintings adorning the walls captured his attention, until a curvy, blonde, army corporal broke the trance with glistening blue eyes and neon-white teeth.

"Good morning, Mr. District Attorney. The general is expecting you. If you will just have a seat right here, he will see you in just a moment. Would you like a cup of coffee, tea, or perhaps a soda?" she offered, adding to the illusion that he was there of his own will.

"A cup of coffee never hurts," he replied with an affable smile. "Black." He was unable to maintain a curt disposition in the face of such a desirable woman. He felt instantly disarmed and wondered if that was part of the plan. He continued to examine the works of art as she went to get his drink. Though he was no art snob, he was impressed with the use of light and the thickness of the paint built up on the canvases. Most were by the same artist, and though he had never heard of him, it was obviously fine art and very expensive for back offices in a warehouse.

When she returned with his coffee, he took a seat on the deep-brushed, suede sofa, being careful not to spill. He waited through fifteen minutes of eye-footsie with the cute corporal before he began to get antsy. Just before he spoke up, she disarmed him again with another smile. After a humbling twenty-five minutes, she approached him. "General Quinn will see you now," she said, as she ushered him through heavily lacquered, cherry-wood double doors into a large private office appointed in shiny, black-lacquered furniture and glass tabletops with chrome fixtures. The dominant feature of the room was a wide, floor-to-ceiling, plate-glass window overlooking a private set of docks on the Oakland shipyard, the bay beyond, and, in the distance across a flat expanse of water, the San Francisco skyline. A large ornate mirror hung on the wall adjacent to the window, reflecting the view and making the room feel even bigger.

The general's desk, a two-inch-thick, beveled-glass top resting
on two, square, onyx-black pillars, faced away from the window, the
high-backed leather chair with its back to the view. The cute corporal
led Simmons to a second matching, high-backed chair just beside the
desk and right in front of the window. She placed his cup neatly on a
coaster atop a knee-high, circular coffee table that separated the two
chairs.

*　*　*　*　*　*　*

Very early the next morning, Kassen and Nolan rousted me from
my holding cell after a very unsatisfying sleep. They were both in a
pretty good mood. I guessed that the idea of getting their hands on
Chet, and possibly all that money, had buoyed their spirits overnight.
They took me straight to the underground garage, where some kind
of tech guy fitted me with a listening device about the size of a deck
of cards with a microphone on a thin wire secreted in the collar of
my shirt. They tested the receiver, and earpieces, and the attached
miniature-cassette recorder. After all was determined to be in order,
they stuffed me into the back of an unmarked police car and headed
for the address listed in Peterson's notes. I really had no idea where
I was going. The fear and anticipation was almost blinding, but the
Narrator in my head tried to calm me as they quizzed me for fifteen
minutes while they circled the neighborhood. I was to be sure to get
Chet to incriminate himself as the leader of the conspiracy and to find
out what had happened to the money. They stopped the car around
the corner from the location for a last check and a final warning that
I had to get what they wanted or face dire consequences. Then they
slowly pulled up across the street from a brick-faced, waterfront
warehouse with attached offices. Kassen and Nolan turned me loose
and pointed me toward a door on the office side of the building. I

walked at a normal pace, but I wanted to run for the door, knowing my salvation lay inside.

As the two D.E.A. cops watched and listened from across the street, a soldier in a marine uniform with master-sergeant stripes opened the door quickly after I knocked. He was very serious looking, and he must have sensed a hug coming because he stepped back, putting a finger to his lips to signal me to be quiet while motioning for me to enter. Once inside, he looked me over and discovering the bug in my collar he gave me the okay sign, and then asked me, out loud, to please follow. He led me to an empty office with a lone fold-up chair that faced the room's only appointment, a curtained wall. Someone brought in a pizza and two bottles of beer from the Mendocino Brewing Company, which I attacked right away. Then Sergeant Smiles parted the curtain to reveal a one-way glass window about four-feet square that looked into a luxurious, water's-edge office with a window on the bay. A man I didn't recognize by his profile was seated at the window drinking a cup of coffee. Sergeant Smiles said in a voice loud enough for Kassen and Nolan to hear, "The gentleman you see there is U.S. Assistant District Attorney Frank Simmons. He can't see or hear you." Then he left me alone.

*       *       *       *       *       *       *

A tall, fit man graying at the edges burst through the door at the far end of the office in full stride, a glad-hand extended from a finely tailored military uniform with a lapel full of dangling war jewelry. "Good day, sir," he greeted his visitor with deference. "I'm General Lance Quinn." Although his handshake was firm and fast, the fingertips and palm were soft and smooth, not at all what one would expect of a military man. His eyes were bright blue, clear and deep like Caribbean waters, and they seemed to lock onto the D.A.'s own eyes. He motioned for Simmons to retake his chair and, swiveling his own chair around to face the water, sat down for what looked more like a cozy chat than a formal dressing-down. "Well, Mr. District Attorney, I don't know how much you know about our little operation here, but we have been looking into your record, and I must say we are quite impressed with your work. The general produced a thick, legal-size, manila folder from his desk with pictures clipped to the inside and a bold-lettered red stamp on the cover that read, "Eyes Only," and began to flip through it. "I was impressed with the way you stood your ground with Colonel Edwards, so I spoke to the attorney general, and though he says you are a little by-the-book, he is glad to have you on his team." Simmons tried to hold onto what was left of his indignation but felt it slipping away. "In fact, we may have a place for you here at N.S.A. We could use a man like you in our unit. Could you use a bump up to a G-8 security clearance and a hefty raise in salary?" He dropped the folder on the coffee table. Simmons wanted to pick it up but knew better. Quinn didn't wait for an answer. "However, before that can happen, we have a few things to discern...," He paused, but Simmons resisted the urge to jump in, preferring to stare right into his questioner's eyes to get the measure of the man. He was unnerved by their twinkling blue color that, when seen at the right angle, faded through opaque to hollow black. More of an absence of light than the color of black ink on the page. "Like your willingness to do what it takes to accomplish a necessary task for your country," Quinn finished.

Truthfully, Simmons, who would never do anything less than legal, was becoming enamored with the promise of more clout and more money that goes along with a trusted position at the National Security Agency. He spoke up for himself, "Given a task worthy of my talent," he squinted his eyes to look more serious, "I can be like a dog on a piece of meat."

"Well, sir, it seems that you are in a position to do a valuable service for your country. Something that will save her from a terrible political embarrassment at the hands of our enemies." His voice lowered and became more theatrical. "Son, I've defended our homeland for going on thirty years now and have never had to ask a fellow compatriot what I'm about to ask you. However, I'm compelled to do so for the sake of our nation, and I'm hoping you will take my request in the same light. You see, unfortunate as it may be..." the general hesitated, "...you have busted one of my boys, and I want... strike that... it is imperative that I get him back."

"Now, I suppose you are talking about your wayward colonel," the A.D.A. said smugly. "I already told your man Edwards..."

"No, no," General Quinn interrupted. "We aren't concerned about the colonel. He is a patriot and an elderly gentleman who should not face prosecution, but he knew the risks and our government can count on him to remain silent. No. This is my man." He removed my picture from the manila folder, where it was clipped to another bogus personnel file. It was a picture Chet had taken of me, in uniform, two years earlier.

I felt like I was watching a movie of my life, and I could only imagine what was going on at the other end of my bug.

Simmons recognized my photo right away. "This dope-growing felon you call 'your man' is involved in a huge grow and refuses to cooperate by implicating the kingpin of the operation, a guy named Hawthorne, or by telling officers where the proceeds went."

"His name is Lieutenant Jason Garrett. He spent four years in the Corps and retired. Then after two years of civilian life, he got popped in a small-time grow, and *we* recruited *him* for this operation.

"You see, Colonel Halston was using the proceeds from this venture to add to the resources of some of our mutual friends in Central America." This was the twist that Chet knew would throw them for a loop, and Quinn could see the gears start cranking behind Simmons's eyes. "The mill could produce millions of dollars to finance under-the-table political operations, but Halston needed help to expand, so we introduced Garrett. We put him in there to keep an eye on things so we would know exactly what was coming out. He's a nobody, but he's our nobody. Do you recognize this man?" The general produced another picture from the secret file, which Simmons knew immediately as the well-known leader and fundraiser for a Contra rebel group.

"Yes, this is Jose Escarpa of the F.A.R.K."

"That is correct. Here I have pictures of him meeting with our boy Garrett and receiving large boxes of Contra-bound money grown in the garden." General Quinn had more pictures of me meeting with other so-called freedom fighters. "Unfortunately for everyone, he knows too much and unlike Colonel Halston he has no incentive to remain silent. He could expose the U.S. government to drug-production and weapons-dealing charges for the purposes of the violent overthrow of a sovereign foreign nation. Besides, he's a small fry who would never have been in there if we hadn't put him there. No, I'm afraid we can't let you have him." He stood and walked to the back of the A.D.A.'s chair.

Simmons could see the general's reflection in the window glass. "You mean to tell me you sell this poison to American kids to fund an illegal war?"

"Don't be naïve!," the general said. He spun the D.A.'s chair around to face him. Simmons immediately saw that the two big, black-suited bruisers had entered the room. Quinn pulled Simmons out of his seat by his lapels, turned him around, and slammed him into the chests of the wall-like giants, right in front of my mirror, then descended on him like a crazed maniac, shouting right in his face. I saw the crazed look on the general's face, and though there wasn't the slightest resemblance, I knew for sure it was Picnic. A chill took up residence in my spine. I never could have imagined that this enigmatic friend from the Hawaiian jungle could morph into the extremely violent man that stood before me. "You must give him to me!" His voice boomed now with ominous import. "While you fight a superfluous war on drugs, like a rat on a wheel, we are trying to save the civilized world from the specter of godless communism! For God's sake man, ours is a fight for democracy! For freedom itself! For the existence of liberty!" His hands were outstretched now and his face shaking as he thundered to a conclusion. "It's a struggle to the death for our very way of life, and you would sacrifice all that for a meager pot bust?"

"So just what is it that you expect me to do?" A.D.A Simmons was scared but incredulous. "I understand your predicament, but this bust was big news around here. I can't just let them go unprosecuted. I've got clean convictions here. I'd be the laughingstock of my profession. Someone has got to go down for this one. What about this Hawthorne guy?"

"You are referring to one Chester Hawthorne?" Quinn said disgustedly.

"Yeah, Chester Hawthorne. You got a picture of him in here?" Simmons opened the manila folder to look but instead was shocked to find pictures of his home, his wife Ann, and his daughter Amy playing in a schoolyard. His heart stopped, and he immediately felt threatened.

General Quinn scooped up the folder and its contents. "There is no such person as Chester Hawthorne," he said.

"Huh?" Simmons couldn't believe it. His head was spinning. The two D.E.A. agents were fuming in their car outside. Nolan was ready to bust in and choke somebody.

"Well, where in the hell did we get that name?" Simmons was filled with a mixture of fear and anger. "We just fuckin' talked to his secretary at the Pentagon," Kassen hissed to his partner.

"Chester Hawthorne is a fictional character we made up so that Halston and Garrett could make contact with the N.S.A. You got it from this guy, the third man your agents picked up at the garden." The master spy was leading this government man around by his nose. He plucked the portrait of his victim out of the manila folder. "This is Patrick Halston, the colonel's son and mastermind behind the whole garden idea." This is where Chet would exact his revenge. "He was growing on a much smaller scale inside the mill, and when his father saw the potential for advancing our cause, he received tacit approval from the highest levels of our government's intelligence apparatus to expand operations at the mill, and that's when we put Garrett in there. The Halston kid is just using this Hawthorne character to try to take the heat off himself."

"Well, I don't know how I'd explain it to the agents in charge. Maybe I can drop the case against your man Garrett, but only if the son agrees to plead to the charges and Colonel Halston makes a statement as a corroborating witness. If he wants to walk away from this, I want some blood!" The government prosecutor actually thought it was his idea.

Picnic had him right where he wanted him. "I think we can convince Colonel Halston that he has to deal. Patrick got him into this jam in the first place, now he can get him out. And don't worry about those two cops. They'll either play along, or I'll have their throats ripped out!" Kassen and Nolan glanced at each other and shifted uncomfortably in their seats. They had been threatened before, but never by a vicious Marine Corps general working in the intelligence underworld.

Simmons tried to ignore the threat, "Okay. We can drop it to a few charges and recommend the minimum. He should do three to five, max." Simmons was happy to be getting a hot body and doing a service for his country. At least, that was the line Picnic was pushing.

The two big agents escorted Simmons first to the limo and then back to the federal building, with his nerves a little shaken but his dignity intact. Picnic fixed his perfect white hair and straightened his collar in the mirror, looking right through me. Then just as I became mesmerized by the depth of his eyes, he winked at me, and before I could respond, Sergeant Smiles came in and closed the curtain. Without a word, he returned me to the street and into the hands of two very confused and pissed-off D.E.A. cops.

Colonel Halston would be only too happy to let his son plead out to a lesser charge that netted him a few years but kept the colonel himself out of the picture. He never really knew what happened. He thought the whole thing was Junior's idea and figured Pat was lucky to get off easy. Simmons would have no problem convincing his higher-ups at justice to let things lie. After all, he had his pound of flesh and another conviction added to his record. Chet finally had his way with Patrick for his earlier betrayal and got paid to boot, just as he said he would.

\* \* \* \* \* \* \*

I spent six-and-a-half days in the dirty pit of a jail in the basement of Oakland's federal building. It was crowded and smelled of perspiration, Lysol, and bad food. It was an all-artificial environment. No windows or natural light, air-conditioned stale air, and no green in sight. The guards acted like sadistic tormentors who never missed a chance to fuck with me. There were no letters from home and no visitors, leaving me a lot of time to think about the road I'd traveled, how many wrong turns I'd made, how close I came to pulling the whole thing off, and where this madness would end up. I had wasted the last few years of my life and was heading for spending the next few behind bars. I'd lost a fortune in cash. The love of my life had abandoned me for my best friend, and Jim was left to fend for himself in a complicated world. It was one big pile of shit. After my experience at the warehouse, I felt pretty sure that everything could work out, but in the days since then, I had begun to worry that maybe Chet had played his hand too strong. Perhaps intimidation had just angered the government men. And then, when it couldn't have looked any bleaker, the key turned in the lock of my cell, sounding like freedom ringing. They took me, confused and bewildered, to a holding cell while they processed the paperwork for my release. I waited all of about an hour before they returned my belongings and turned me loose with no explanation.

It was hard to contain my glee when I cleared the big glass doors and my feet hit the pavement. I looked around, wondering which direction to start in. A cool breeze blowing from the north seemed to push me toward the south. I began to stroll, feeling as free as the wind. I was broke as the wind, too, but that didn't matter. I didn't get as far as the corner before a speeding vehicle came to a screeching halt just behind my left shoulder, causing me to jump. Looking back, I saw the sweetest sight I'd ever seen. The Mobile Hilton, all shiny and spit-polished like new. From behind the wheel, Chester Hawthorne, grinning like a hyena, leaned over toward the passenger window. "What'd I tell ya!?" he shouted and began to laugh like I had never seen. "Who's the man?"

"You definitely the man!" I had to give him that.

He got out of the car and handed me the keys. "Good, then you'll be ready the next time I need you." I didn't answer. He flagged the very first taxi and was gone.

The Narrator was dying to rip open the stash, but I didn't even check to see if my three million in cash and five pounds of supreme Elvis hash was still hidden in the paneled walls. My luck was running too good to question it. I just drove straight to the Port of Oakland and dropped the van off with a shipper who would deliver it to Kawaihai on the Big Island in three weeks. I'd be there in time to meet it.